# Apollo

**Olivia Schimtd**

# Contents

# Chapter One

----------------------------------------

LOCKHART MANOR TREMBLED WITH THE NOISE OF AB-SOLUTE QUIET NOW that Emmeline was gone from it. The entirety of Portsmouth missed her, but no one more than her twin brother. Emmett Lockhart spent most of his days in his study with his head in his hands, wondering what he had done. His actions were driven by a will to stop himself from losing the two people closest to his heart; yet they had done just the opposite, and now because of the mistakes he had made he would not have both in his life half as frequently as he would like to. Emmeline lived in St James' Palace, which was a day and a half away. Peter, in the meantime, had turned to the ocean in a search for respite from his heart-break, and his request to his superiors to be deployed to patrol the colonies was quickly granted with a nod and a sympathetic look in the rear admiral's eye.

It was just as he had feared: Earl Portsmouth was all alone.

Sighing, he returned his eyes to the envelope before him. It was from his father. Despite offering his support should the young lord ever seek it, William had chosen not to write him for a long while, hoping to give him time to nurse his own broken soul instead of bombarding him with plans to find him a wife or with London noise so quickly after Emmeline's wedding. The old duke had done so rightly, and Emmett had appreciated his consideration, but it now seemed like his period of rest from the many complexities of high society was over. Breaking the wax seal open, he pulled out the letter and began to read.

Dear Emmett

I hope you have somewhat recovered. I understand that you remain very upset by Emmeline's marriage and Captain Jamison's departure, and it is because of all the complications with your sister's affairs that I have put this off for many months. However, son, remember that your own marriage continues to be an issue I need to resolve.

I think we have confirmed this earlier in the year: Lady Adelaide Farthingale does not seem to be an option for you. As such, I have written my friend the Duke of Westchester, who has a lovely daughter Victoria. From what Lord Westchester has told me, I think you might be fond of her. Do come to Wellington House, and we will discuss it in person. I will be expecting you.

Yours William Lockhart

Sighing once again, he pulled open his drawer to find a piece of letter paper and an envelope before penning his reply immediately, thanking William for his concern but, in the same breath, notifying his father that he had no will to travel into the city over his marriage – that, in fact, he had no will to marry at all. He wrote that he hoped William would grant his wish and leave him in peace just for one more month and signed off before sealing his envelope, writing William's particulars on it before handing it to a servant to be mailed. The butler cast a worried look his way, but took his leave without comment and sent the letter on its way to Wellington House.

Emmett's position on marriage had not changed: he was against it. He did not wish to marry. Previously, he had taken such a stand for pride and rebellion's sake, also inspired by his own parents' broken relationship. Now, however, his aversion to marital union originated not from angst or hatred but from deep regret and remorse. The one person he loved more than any on the face of the earth, his sister, would never be with the man she loved. She would be trapped in a marriage she did not want for decades, perhaps until her last breathing day, caged in the way their mother Anne had been for the entirety of her life...and it was all because of him.

If this was so, perhaps he did not deserve a blissful marriage either. He had ruined his sister's life. How could he allow himself to find happiness while his sister would forever be chained to a man she did not love, all because of his folly? How would he live with himself? He already felt as if his guilt devoured him every day. He did not wish to add to the list of actions he hated himself for.

A glance at the time revealed that he had an appointment with some of the Portsmouth gentry over a small affair he could not recall the intricacies of. He rose and proceeded toward his drawing room. When his visitors arrived, they exchanged a surprised glance at how much Earl Portsmouth had changed – his green eyes, usually lively and even slightly mischievous, had faded considerably, and looked tired and worn. His usually charming smile seemed forced, and as he shook their hands, he seemed absolutely exhausted by all the events in his life.

Yet it seemed as if his efficiency remained unchanged – in fact, with all his playfulness gone, he might just have been speedier than ever at resolving the issue, and the trio managed to sort through the issue in only slightly over an hour. The earl promised to look into their affair further after they had taken their leave, and they thanked him profusely before starting for the door.

One of the gentlemen, however, could not resist his urge to express some form of concern for this young lord. Emmett had always been extremely amiable and diligent in his duties, and most of the Portsmouth townsfolk were rather fond of him. Hence many were saddened by knowledge of the pain he was going through, and this particular one, who had seen his face and felt his grief first-hand, felt a strong compulsion to try to offer some comfort. He turned and smiled sadly at Lord Portsmouth.

"Take care, milord."

He did not know if Emmett understood the subtext of his words as he nodded briskly with a faint smile. "I will, Sir, thank you; vice versa. Expect a letter within the week."

The guests thanked him once again before finally leaving, and Emmett returned to his study, where he promptly began to leaf through some documents related to their case which he found in one of his cabinets. His mind threatened to wander to his sister and all the guilt, grief and other preoccupations that came with thoughts of her. He cleared his head with a slight shake of his head before delving back into his work, his only guiltless respite from the pain he faced every day.

Serving the people of Portsmouth used to be a pleasure. Now, it was a necessity.

***

SITTING IN HIS DRAWING ROOM MANY MILES AWAY FROM PORTSMOUTH, Duke William Mayfair shook his head with a sigh as his dark eyes flitted over his son's spidery hand. Truth be told, he had already expected that he would receive such a reply, though his expectations did differ vastly from his hopes. They often did. The letter indicated, quite stubbornly, that Emmett would not come to London – William had known it for a long time.

He looked up to gaze out the window. His garden, now trimmed to a presentable extent by a gardener Emmeline had insisted he hire, was perhaps somewhat more pleasing to the eye. Sunlight spilled through dense clouds to land on the shrubbery and trees in streams. Flowers lent specks of bright colour to lush shades of green. If he closed his eyes, William could still see envision his daughter walking through the garden, inspecting progress with her sharp green eyes as she periodically told the gardeners to trim a bush or reshape a tree, to fertilise a plant or plant more flowers in a particular plot of land.

The drawing room, on the other hand, was aglow with the lamps his late wife had left behind. He had not lit for many years after her death, but his daughter, before her marriage, had ordered his servants to light them every day. William had, back then, feigned unwillingness and pretended to grumble, but in sooth he knew that his daughter's restorations had brightened his days significantly now that the house he lived in no longer reeked of death. The refurbishments had been her parting gifts to him, a way of goodbye, and while it pleased him to know she cared for him so, the notion of her departure to St James' Palace made his heart clench.

His daughter – she had been crowned a princess, and though she had smiled out of courtesy on her coronation day, he knew that she was only masking her pain. He had seen the tears in her eyes during her wedding, and he knew that she had had little respite from her sadness even as the days passed since that day. Of course, being Emmeline Lockhart, she comforted him frequently despite the fact that she was, in truth, the one trapped in an unhappy marriage. In her correspondence and during his visits, she had promised him many a time that her life was not as horrible as they had imagined it might be, but he still did feel guilty. Whatever she took the pains to say to him, he knew all too well that he had failed her. With every passing day, he hated more and more his inability to secure her the only marriage she truly wanted, for it had been the only thing she had ever asked of him in many years.

He sighed. He knew that he already owed much to her.

He picked up his pen and found a fresh sheet of writing paper. Only he was not crafting a reply to his son.

Now he would owe her more yet.

***

THERE WAS A RAP ON THE DOOR. "YOUR HIGHNESS?"

"Come in." Emmeline sounded bored. She sat in her study, staring blankly out a window at the perfectly groomed palace gardens. A slight frown had nestled itself in a gentle curve on her ruby lips as she wondered if some wildflowers here and there would make the garden look any less dead.

"Your Highness, there is a letter for you – from His Grace Duke Mayfair."

Upon hearing this news, Emmeline turned in her chair with such abruptness that her crown nearly fell off her head. Steadying it with her hand with no attempt to restore her image of dignified grace, she exclaimed, "Well, then pray let me have it!"

Bowing partly out of propriety and partly to hide an amused smile, the servant obliged, handing her the wax-sealed envelope and retreating from the room. He would leave the princess alone with her excitement and the letter from her father – all staff members in the palace knew how much she missed her family, spending all her time waiting for them to write her like a caged bird waiting for salvation.

Emmeline, in the meantime, tore the envelope open as if she had been deprived of correspondence for a long time – which she had not, for her father had been writing her frequently, and after her rise to royalty all the girls who had once shunned her were now begging her to come to tea with them – and pulled out the letter, her eyes flying over the words. Her brow creased as she read. Was her brother still trapped in his depressed state? He had not visited her for a long time, but he wrote to her regularly, and from his letters she had deduced that his guilt and grief had, mostly, left him... An image of him seated at his desk, forcing a jolly tone in his correspondence while his heart remained in smithereens, entered Emmeline's mind, inducing a deep-reaching ache in her breast. She swallowed. Did he look tired? Like a broken man? How were his spirits?—Surely he had not taken to spirits? Was her brother all right?

She had to see him. But if her father – his father – could not call him to London he might not agree to her request to meet with him either.

The next day, a royal missive arrived at Lockhart Manor's doorstep.

Earl Portsmouth had been summoned to see Her Royal Highness the Princess.

***

# Chapter Two

--------------------------------------------------------

T HE SIGHT OF THE PALACE ONLY SERVED TO BREAK EMMETT LOCKHART'S heart anew. It was the gilded cage he had pushed his sister into – he had turned the lock and swallowed the key, and for all his worth, he had not been able to pull her out of the contraption he had landed her in to begin with.

"Good day, Lord Portsmouth," a palace guard standing near the doors greeted, "Her Royal Highness expects you in her study. I will send for an escort—"

"No need," Emmett interrupted with a sigh, his heart heavy and his tone betraying this. "Thank you. I know the way."

"Very well, Your Lordship." The guard said nothing more as he bowed out of nothing more than courtesy, his voice showing no emotion.

Not caring to add any further comment either, the earl walked past him and into the palace. There was much to admire in the castle's architecture, but he paid the splendour no mind, his step purposeful as he sought to see his sister. She had sent him a summons, a measure he would not have thought necessary, for he would come if she made the slightest indication that she wished him to do so. Yet whatever she had to discuss must be urgent, and so he navigated the halls as quickly as he could. He found her study without much difficulty, and knocked on the door to indicate his presence. He heard her permission for him to enter, and he pushed the door open.

"Emmy!" Her voice and her arms reached him before her image could, and he had not even had the chance to see Emmeline's face when he was wrapped up in her warm embrace. He heard her crown clattering to the ground, and saw it a distance from their feet, but she paid it no mind as she withdrew slightly from him to present him with a glorious smile.

"How have you been, brother?"

"I am well...and you?"

"Well," she parroted. "Come and sit, Emmett, and shall I call for some tea?"

"Tea sounds excellent, Linnie. Let us sit."

She sat, and watched him expectantly with a faint smile. Instead of finding his chair, however, he moved to pick up her abandoned crown before advancing towards her and placing it gently on her head. Then he observed her for a moment, noticing not only that her crown resembled a halo on an angel's jet-black hair but that royalty had lent her regality, and more so than before he was inclined to feel a deep sense of pride at what a lady his sister had become. No, no longer a lady – a princess!

A princess who would never call the man she loved her husband.

Emmett's heart clenched.

She was not happy. He knew it.

It was all his fault.

Before he could let his thoughts consume him and drag him in a downward spiral, however, she took the crown from her head and placed it on the table before her, smiling at him with a glimmer in her eye.

"I am no princess in your presence, Emmett," she explained, "only your sister. Now sit, and I will call for the finest tea St James has to offer."

Emmett complied and Emmeline held up her end of the bargain; within minutes the tea she spoke of was served with scones and crumpets and slices of cake. He watched his sister as she turned to beam at the young girl who was placing the full plates on the table and then pouring the steaming beverage into the two small cups. She was clearly pleased by the tea the kitchens had offered, and her satisfaction did not surprise him in the least. He himself was able to smell the tea and every kind of food on the table, and, he thought, he could almost see the scones waving enticingly at him.

When the younger girl finished arranging the plates and straightened with an empty tray in her hand, Emmeline spoke. Her smile, Emmett noticed, had not taken its leave. "Thank you, Penny. Send my compliments to the chef."

"It was my pleasure, my lady, and I will do so immediately."

He raised his eyes to see the familiar servant – now no longer a servant, he had heard, but a lady-in-waiting pronounced part of the gentry by his sister herself. She smiled in greeting. Emmett recognised the light in her eyes, and he remembered the reason Emmeline was so attached to this lass.

"Your Lordship." She dropped into a curtsy.

"Good day, Miss Smith. Do rise."

"Thank you, my lord." Penelope straightened and smiled at him once more. "It is lovely indeed to see you again, Lord Portsmouth, but I must be on my way."

Reflexively offering a polite response he did not quite hear himself say, he allowed her a ghost of a smile as she bobbed a brief curtsy in Emmeline's direction before scampering off.

"So, Emmy," Emmeline finally said once the sound of Penelope's footsteps has gone from their ears, "I was hoping to speak to you about a Lady Victoria Arden, from Westchester."

A look of recognition came unto his face, and his eyes seemed to light up and darken simultaneously. "Oh, I see what this is about." He sighed heavily. "Emmeline, I have informed Father, many a time in fact, that—"

"—that you do not wish to marry her," she interrupted flatly, reaching for a scone and placing it on his plate. Then she selected a crumpet for herself and leaned back in her chair. "You know I will always be supportive of your wishes if you do decide in the end that they are right and good, Emmett, but would it not be unfair to dismiss Lady Victoria without so much as a glance at her?"

"Thank you," he said, with reference to the scone on his plate, as he picked up the pastry and bit into it. It was every bit as delicious as it looked, he noticed, but he found himself unable to enjoy it with the topic of his unwanted marriage weighing on his mind. As he chewed on the scone he thought about how to answer her question, and when he swallowed, he had the reply he sought to give. "I am not dismissing her, sister, I am dismissing the notion of a wife."

"Please, you cannot do so," she implored, green eyes turning a shade darker in the gravity of the words she spoke. "I know you have always been in opposition of marrying, but time is passing and...You know this already, Emmett – the Lockhart family requires an heir. Any child I would bear would take the last name of St James. You must have a son. It is the only way."

Her earnest plea, however, only earned a sip of tea and a challenging-ly-arched eyebrow from him. "And when, pray tell, did you become interested in marriage and heirs?"

"I am most certainly not," she said, sounding almost offended. This drew a chuckle from Emmett, perhaps meant to further antagonise her, but she only cleared her throat indignantly and continued with her explanation in response. "I am not interested, as you say, in marriage and heirs, but – but Father is. I would hardly care a jot if you should remain a bachelor all your life, but Father worries—he fears that—" She closed her eyes briefly, perhaps involuntarily, as she swallowed a lump that had taken shape in her throat. "He worries that he might not live to see you married with children. It would be his one great regret."

Sighing, Emmett turned away. His father's one great regret. Had he not already done far more than his part in the way of creating regrets for those he loved? Perhaps, not for his own sake but for his family's, he should meet with a Lady Victoria... Perhaps he should not be so selfish for once in his life. He felt guilt puncture his heart, and he swallowed instinctively.

Emmeline had not originally intended to strike a chord so deep within him with her confession of her father's pessimistic concerns, but the genuine worry in her eyes for the elderly duke seemed sufficient for Emmett to reconsider his position. He sighed again as he turned to meet her troubled emerald gaze once more, nodding resignedly. "Very well, then... I will see her, Emmeline, as you wish me to."

"Oh!" His sister was so overcome with emotion at his concession that she cried out with joy, her hands flying to rest upon her cheeks in delight and surprise. "Oh, Emmett, I can hardly—! Thank you! Father will be so pleased!"

He cracked a smile. "No, no, Linnie, you have naught to thank me for."

He paused to reach over the table to pick up a slice of fruit cake and bit into it, chewing ruminatively, before finally asking the question on his tongue. "Come now, tell me about you, sister; tell me about your life. How have you been? Truthfully."

"Truthfully, I have been quite fine," she said, "albeit slightly bored. Palace food is lovely, and the dresses made here are exquisite, but you must call far more often, Emmy. And I would be so pleased if you would with bring you proposals of activities I might engage my mind in, or I think might lose it altogether."

"I shall," he promised, relieved not to hear any devastating complaint from her after the months she had spent in the palace. "How has His Highness been?—Does he treat you as he should?"

Her brow creased and she cocked her head slightly, an amused smile hanging from her lips. "Pray tell, how exactly should a prince treat a wife forced unto him? He does not speak to me often, nor does he seek me out, but he is polite and courteous when he does encounter me, and I am thankful enough for his respect."

He paused. "I apologise, Emmeline, I really am sorry. If not for me—"

With a sigh that indicated exasperation, she cut him off quite abruptly.

"I will be honest and candid with you about my relationship with His Highness, brother, instead of feeding you stories of a fantastical marriage, but you must not feel guilty for it – unless you should want me to stop telling you the truth." She stopped to sigh slightly, the irritation disappearing from her demeanour and a gentle reassuring smile coming onto her face to replace it. "I have accepted my situation, Emmett, and while I am not happy, I am not unhappy either. You were forgiven months ago, Emmett, I beg of you, apologise no more."

He was silent for a long while, his sister's words ricocheting in his mind as he paid every syllable the closest attention, absorbing this information and searching for a response. Finally he did answer her, his voice quiet and his eyes windows to his grieving heart.

"Linnie... You should not have to live thus a life."

"Perhaps not – perhaps you are right," she responded, a melancholy light glistening in the kindest eyes Emmett had ever seen as a patient smile danced across her lips, "but this is my reality, Emmett. I do indeed have to live thus a life, and whether it is just or not I have chosen not to consider any further. It has never done me any good, and it will do you none, either."

✳✳✳

# Chapter Three

A /N Hey everyone! Here's this week's update – TGIF, am I right? :DD

THE COCKEREL SIGNALLED THE BEGINNING OF A NEW DAY, AND DUKE William Mayfair found himself awakening in a good mood. Today was the day the family would dine with Victoria Arden, the lass who, to him, bore promises of his son's marriage and heirs for the Lockhart clan. His daughter had succeeded – and it was just as he had expected. Her perceptiveness and her wit were her finest qualities, and he knew that she would never fail him.

Lord Daniel Arden, his wife Lady Georgeanne and their daughter were due to arrive in Wellington House at noon for luncheon with the their Mayfair counterparts. Emmeline had promised to leave the palace and travel to the manor for the meal. After an afternoon of activities, the princess would proceed with the Lady Victoria to St James' Palace, where she would dine alone with her at dinnertime to assess the prospective bride's character in further detail. William, however, was not worried at all that Emmeline would find any fault with her, for he held high hopes for this match. Daniel Arden was a dear friend, and his daughter would be an excellent choice for Emmett. From what he had heard, the young lady was poised, confident, and graceful – the perfect woman by societal standards. His son would do well to choose her as his bride.

William washed and dressed before proceeding to the dining room to break his fast. He was pleased to find a plate of eggs and meats already waiting before his seat and no one else in the room; he quite liked to have some quiet in the mornings. Unfortunately, his peace was short-lived, for not long after his sixth bite there came a rap on the door followed by the entrance of one of his footmen.

"My apologies for disturbing your meal, Your Grace, but His Lordship Earl Portsmouth has arrived. He is in the drawing room."

A glance at the grandfather clock by the furnace showed that the boy was an hour early. William nodded anyway and gave instructions for Emmett to be directed into the dining room instead, and when the footman left he took his seventh bite of food and thought about what he would have to say to his son in preparation for luncheon.

A few things had come to mind and he was taking his tenth bite when he heard the earl clear his throat by the door. "Good morning, Father. May I come in?"

"Pray do," William replied, "and please sit."

Emmett obliged before speaking again. "I apologise for disturbing your breakfast, Father, I know you do love the quiet."

"It is no matter, Emmett. It is good to see you again." William offered a ghost of a smile. "Have some tea, son, it is your favourite kind."

He looked about the room, but seeing as there were no servants in the room to pour it, Emmett picked up the teapot and helped himself to a cup. Raising the china to his lips, he took a sip almost hesitantly, as if he were afraid to drink. However he found himself his eyes closing involuntarily to heighten his sense of taste as he, reflexively, hummed his appreciation with a slight nod. It seemed to be the best thing his tongue had tasted in far too long. He put the cup back down and offered William a faint smile.

"You are right, Father. It is indeed." He had not drunk this in weeks – with his sister no less than incarcerated in her fancy lodgings he had not had the heart to enjoy even the simplest of life's pleasures, and had nearly forgotten how much he had loved life itself before he had destroyed his sister's.

His sister—"When did Linnie say she would arrive?"

William himself drew a long sip of earl grey, his eyebrows knitted together in thought. He swallowed thickly before answering. "Well, son, I'm afraid she did not specify a time. She did, however, mention arriving ahead of luncheon to ensure that all arrangements are satisfactory – perhaps, then, around eleven?"

Emmett glanced at the clock. Two hours.

His face must have fallen, for his father chuckled amusedly when he noticed the young earl's expression. "Do you miss her already? I will remind you that you did see her just last week."

"Well, I will remind you, Father, that she is my sister," he said, some boyish indignation in his tone as he sat just a fraction straighter in his chair. "I always miss her when she is away from me. I know that it may not seem very becoming, but I love her dearly and I will not hide it."

William directed a brief but uncharacteristically gentle smile at him before shifting his gaze to the remnants of his breakfast and pushing a few slivers of scrambled egg onto his fork. For one very fleeting moment, when they looked into each other's eyes, father and son had connected on a spiritual level still slightly foreign to them. After he had sent the egg on its merry way down his throat, William sighed to himself.

"I know, son; I know."

***

"YOUR GRACE; YOUR LORDSHIP! PRINCESS EMMELINE WILL BE ARRIVING shortly!" A footman announced, sounding rather excited himself as he rushed into the library. Emmeline was, after all, known to often be popular amongst servants and other common folk. "Her Royal Highness sent a man ahead to inform you of it. The carriage will enter the estate in a few minutes."

"Well, then, let us go to greet her, Father!"

Emmett was on his feet before William could put down his book. The duke chuckled in amusement at his child's eagerness to go, but closed the tome and rose from his chair nonetheless.

When the princess's carriage door opened, two of the three men she loved most in the world were standing before her, and her face split into a grin that stretched from ear to ear. She was already ready for the meeting, dressed in elegant silver satin that wrapped tightly around her corset but fell looser past her waist. The layered skirt of her dress was satin and crepe, just barely touching the floor in front but slightly longer behind her. White gloves covered her hands, made of the finest silk in the land. Her face was powdered, rouge staining her cheeks and eyelashes darkened. She wore her hair in a chignon, rounding up her appearance with a sparkling silver tiara. She did look like a princess, William marvelled. His daughter had grown into such a beautiful woman.

"Father! Brother!" she cried, jumping off the carriage and into Emmett's arms. The black-haired earl whirled her around in a circle, her skirts flying and laughter bubbling out of her throat. *Perhaps she is not quite yet a* woman, Duke Mayfair thought with a soft smile, still very much my little girl. Quite accustomed to the liberal nature of this family, the footmen did not seem to mind very much. When he set her down again, she curtsied deeply to her father, who bowed slightly in return before drawing her into a warm hug.

"Oh, I do look forward to meeting the Ardens," she gushed with an excited giggle. "Is everything in order, Father?" Then, before William had a chance to answer, she shook her head to stop him and took his elbow in her hand. "Oh, never mind, you should just show me instead."

With a critical emerald eye, Emmeline checked every platter of food, every wine goblet, and every decoration in every room in the house. "Everything must be absolutely perfect," she kept saying with her eyes alight, "Emmett's future depends on how successful this meal is."

Before, Bethany Rutherford would have been the one in charge of inspecting the house, but today the task fell to Princess Emmeline since her aunt had decided it was time for her to take on more womanly responsibilities in the Lockhart clan. She, however, suspected another reason for the conspicuous absence of Bethany's fussing: she was avoiding William, whom she clearly was not the fondest of and who was becoming far more involved in his children's lives since misunderstandings had been diffused and apologies had been made. Nonetheless, out of concern for her nephew, Bethany would be present for luncheon with the Westchester nobles.

She arrived just before the other family was due to, dressed in purple and looking as pleased with herself as ever. Emmeline and Emmett greeted her with an intimate embrace each, the younger twin gushing about how long it had been since they last met. She ignored William's curt nod, electing instead to ask after her niece's life in the palace.

"Is it every bit as wonderful as I knew it would be?"

Emmeline smiled, far more easily than she expected herself to. "Not quite, Aunt Bethany." She hesitated, but caught herself, swallowed the ball of fear in her throat and decided to speak boldly – she was, after all, no longer the wary lass she used to be. All the misery of her new life had been bestowed unto her by her tendency to keep mum, and it had taught her to do better than say nothing. She had paid the price for her shortcomings, and she was determined not to make the same mistakes over and over again in what she had left of her life. She was no longer a girl. She was a true lady now. No – a princess.

"St James is a beautiful place, Aunt, but I live in something of a cage."

"I don't understand, my darling," Bethany said, her brow knitting together tightly. "Does His Highness treat you poorly? I will write Sarah once I—"

"No! No." The princess hurried to dispel any myths about her husband. "Alexander is... He is not unfair to me. He tries...he treats me civilly. But he does not love me. He does not want to be married to me." She laughed dryly, turning away from her wide-eyed aunt. "I can hardly blame him. I do not want to be married to him, either."

Bethany exhaled, then inhaled and made to speak, but stopped again.

Finally she said something, her voice cautious and gentle. "Emmeline... Emmeline, you are happy, are you not?"

She faced the older woman, squaring her shoulders and letting a ghost of a smile settle upon her ruby lips. "No, Aunt, I am not. I am married to a man I do not love and the man I do love has sailed far away from grief." She swallowed. "But I will blame no one but myself. If I were any true lady back then, I would have stood up for myself. I..." She paused. "I should have been better."

Bethany frowned.

Had she erred?

***

# Chapter Four

--------------------------------------------------

"GOOD DAY, DAVID! GOOD DAY, LADY VICTORIA." WILLIAM LOCKHART WAS positively beaming when his friend and his daughter emerged from their carriage to step onto the driveway. "Where is Lady Georgeanne? I thought she was to accompany you."

"Good day indeed, William." Grinning broadly, the Duke of Westchester shook his hand heartily. "I'm afraid my wife is rather unwell today... She did appear to be quite all right yesterday, but this morning she woke up and said she had a dreadful headache. But it matters not – I am quite sure her illness will be gone as soon as it came." He turned to smile tenderly at his child before introducing her to his friend. "William, this is my beloved daughter Victoria. Victoria, my darling, this is my most esteemed friend Duke William Mayfair."

"Good day, Your Grace," she said breezily, only bothering to gaze briefly at her potential future father-in-law before turning her back to the pavement as she bent her knees slightly in an excuse for a curtsy. Apparently, the cobblestone was more worthy of her attentions than the Duke of Mayfair.

William's delighted expression crumpled immediately, his brow furrowing at her for a moment, but with a heavy exhale forced himself to quell his irritation quickly. This lass was, after all, his friend's daughter, and while she may be disrespectful, he had no wish to be rude to David.

"Good day, Lady Victoria." All his previous warmth evaporated and politeness remaining solely by manner of force, he offered her a stiff bow before turning to his Westchester counterpart. Some emotion returned to his face, though it did still look strained. "She is indeed lovely, David. Allow me to introduce my sister-in-law, Marchioness Bethany Rutherford of Whitehall."

Bethany curtsied. "A pleasure, Your Grace."

"The pleasure is ours, Your Ladyship. A very good day to you." David, not seeming to notice William's chagrin, bowed in return with a merry chuckle. Finally recognising someone of her calibre, his haughty daughter sank into an impressively low curtsy.

"Good day, Your Ladyship."

"Oh! You are so wonderfully well-mannered, Lady Victoria," the older noblewoman gushed in utter elation, her face lighting up. "I'm sure Emmett will be terribly fond of you. He awaits us in the dining room – he is keeping his sister company, you understand."

"If she is unable to await me alone, why do they not both greet us outside?"

Bethany seemed slightly surprised by the question, eyebrows lifting and lips parting slightly. From her manner and her diction, there was no question that the Westchester girl knew propriety – yet she asked a question Bethany would have expected to come out of the mouth of an ignorant country bumpkin.

Nonetheless, she plastered her polite smile back on her face after an impressively short time, offering the young lady something of an explanation – but more of an opportunity to recover and save face.

"My niece is the princess, Lady Victoria, surely you do not expect royalty to stand outside in the middle of winter to greet you?"

Oh, of course not, Madam, my apologies, was the answer Bethany had expected. Then the older woman would laugh the whole thing off, the girl would offer a sheepish smile, and they would all be on their merry way to luncheon. Instead, Victoria elected to raise a pointed eyebrow and reply,

"Respectfully, Madam, is she not a host? Should hosts not greet their guests?"

The young lady's hostility caught Bethany off guard. She had never seen a daughter of a duke so young and so beautiful, and yet with so much bite in her words. She stood staring at her, not knowing what she could possibly say that would mend the situation.

"Respectfully, Lady Victoria, she is not here as your host," William was quick to step in and make a retort on his sister-in-law's behalf. How could his dear friend have raised such an impertinent, demanding child? Perhaps it had something to do with her curiously absent mother... "My sister and I are. Her Royal Highness is attending this meal as Earl Portsmouth's sister, and a guest in this house. I'm certain you remember that she no longer lives here – she is currently residing in St James's Palace."

"Of course, Sir," she replied begrudgingly, still wearing an unconvinced frown on her face although not daring to make any more remarks about Emmeline Lockhart given William's clear vexation.

Clearing her throat to collect herself once more – as any proper lady should in such a situation – Bethany straightened and directed a smile at a rather nervous-looking Duke Westchester, carefully ignoring his haughty daughter. She had never once in her life encountered such a self-important and incorrigible young lady – filled with such arrogance that even after

William had issued his firm statement she looked displeased with the whole arrangement.

"Shall we proceed to the dining room, Your Grace? Our wonderful chef Adalberto has a rather splendid meal waiting for us on the table, and it would be a capital shame to let it go cold."

"Yes, Lady Bethany, that sounds like a delightful idea." He turned to Victoria with a smile, either not noticing how offensive she was or being too indulgent of a father to address it. "Come now, my darling."

"Yes, Papa." Her answer was meek and sweet, not a trace of venom in her words, and William understood why David doted on her so.

William and Bethany led the two guests to the dining room, where Emmeline was seated to the left of the head of the table and Emmett was sitting next to her. The most important seat belonged to William, and the one on its right was to be David's for the day.

"Children," William greeted. "The guests have arrived – Duke David Westchester and his daughter Lady Victoria Arden."

Both siblings stood to greet them. Emmett bowed graciously to them both. "Your Grace. My lady."

The greying duke bowed in return. "Ah, Earl Portsmouth. I have heard much about you – and I will say that I am impressed. Not more than twenty and five and already well known across the kingdom as an outstanding earl."

He chuckled. "You have my thanks for bearing such a high opinion of me, Sir, but I am hardly worthy."

"You are humble, as well, I see," David remarked with delight in his eyes before turning to the princess and bowing deeply. "And a very good day to you, Your Royal Highness."

Victoria sank into a low curtsy as well, although not saying anything.

Emmeline curtsied in return, smiling courteously. "Good day indeed, Duke Westchester; do rise. Thank you, and your daughter, for coming today. I must tell you that I have heard much about your exceptional administration from my husband and his family – and His Majesty King Andrew sends his regards." Her emerald eyes flitted away from the slightly roundish man as she beamed at her aunt and father. "Well, then, shall we all sit? We have quite a lovely meal ahead of us."

"Oh, yes, of course, let us sit!" Looking beyond pleased with Emmeline's little speech, Bethany took her position beside her nephew. William found his chair at the head of the table and Victoria sat demurely down next to her father. Duke Mayfair called for the dishes to be served, and servants began to stream into the room with fresh bread rolls.

"So, Lady Victoria." William initiated the table conversation. "What are your interests?—Do you play music, sing, draw, paint, write...?"

"I do them all," she replied, tilting her chin upwards as she looked down at him with a shadow of scorn in her chocolate-hued eyes. "Papa invests quite heavily in my extracurriculars. He wishes me to be all-rounded."

Both Lockhart twins noticed her manner, and Emmett cast his eyes toward his plate as a slight frown found its way to his sister's face.

"What about you, Earl Portsmouth?" David asked, sounding eager or perhaps just anxious. "What interests do you have?"

"I have been particularly busy with my duties to Portsmouth as of late, Your Grace," he replied in half-truths. "But I do use my spare moments reading should they arise, rare as they might be."

"Truly, you enjoy to read? What genre?" the older man asked, interest tinting the edges of his question.

"I quite enjoy reading non-fiction," he said. This answer was not exactly what Emmeline had expected, and was no light in his eyes, she noticed as she watched him speak. Her heart sank – she knew him well enough to know that he was speaking his confession, that he was telling the story of his guilt and grief. "I used to like fiction as well, but lately I have found myself failing to derive much pleasure from it."

Her heart sank even deeper into her chest.

"Is that so? Why might that be?"

"Oh, let me, Your Lordship, I do believe I know your answer!" Victoria offered with a thrilled smile when Emmett opened his mouth to respond.

Mostly disinterested in the conversation anyway and only having said so much to Duke Westchester for the sake of courtesy, the young earl nodded his permission. "Of course, my lady."

Emmeline leaned forward slightly. The lass was, no doubt, intending to flaunt her sophistication or intelligence with this subject, and she was interested to hear what she had to say about it. After all, this Victoria could never possibly know what Emmett was about to say. She hardly knew the man, and there was no way she could know of his story – or, judging by her affected way, she would not have bothered to be in attendance for luncheon.

The princess, of course, was right. With a rather vexatious glint in her eye that bordered on being smug, Lady Victoria proceeded to say, "I too find works of fiction absolutely pointless. It is, after all, only a matter of pretend and of the imagination. If reading is for knowledge, why read something that is hardly even real?"

"I beg to differ, Lady Victoria. I actually find fiction quite informative." Emmeline looked as witheringly she she could at the other young woman as she made her counterargument. The rebuttal was, after all, meant as a means to test the Westchester girl's mettle. "Do you not think that the perspectives that fiction is able to bring to the table are reflections of society past and present? Are the views, priorities, dreams, and fears of the people naught but 'absolutely pointless' to you?"

"Of course not," Victoria snapped, before realising that she had lashed out at the wife of the future king and hastily collecting herself with a wounded sniff and rephrasing her statement. "Of course they are not. I care for the people very much. Their opinion matters to me greatly...as it does to my father."

"Pray tell me then, why does it matter to you?"

"I...well, I think—it simply does..., Your Highness," she choked out. "Per—Perhaps my father would have a better answer for you. Papa?"

"Ah, er, yes, of course." The far more worldly duke, of course, had no issue answering the question, but he – as much as Victoria – knew that she had failed the test the princess had administered. "The people matter to me, Your Royal Highness, because they are my people. Just as their allegiance is to me, mine is to them...and, if I were to speak more liberally, I might even consider myself their steward – for to lead is to serve, is it not?"

"Why, yes, Duke Westchester," Emmeline agreed with a smile. She glanced at his daughter with some disdain in her eyes before returning her attentions to him, the warmth returning to her demeanour. "I agree wholeheartedly. If not for the people, we would not have any power, and it is thusly our duty to use our authority to serve them the best we can...and how would we do so if we did not even know the manner in which we see the world?"

"Precisely, Madam." Although his opinion had won the princess's approval, he did not seem very comfortable. He cast an uneasy look in William's direction, who simply sighed with a barely noticeable shake of his head. Both men knew the chances of their children marrying stood at slim to none now.

***

A/N Hi everyone! Happy Friday! Thank you as always for reading – do vote and comment because it really means so much to me <3 tell me what you thought about Victoria and her dad – as well as her very noticeably absent mother, and the next chapter will be out next week! :) x Leanne

# Chapter Five

-----------------------------------------------



"I THOROUGHLY DISLIKE THE GIRL," EMMELINE SAID WHEN HER MAID-IN-waiting asked her opinion of the Westchester lass she was about to dine privately with. "She is more snobbish than my Aunt Bethany and not as wise as she fancies herself. This will be my final test for her – but I am already quite certain that I will never allow her to marry my brother."

"Well," Penelope sighed as she pulled her mistress's hair into a braid, "if you dislike her so, my lady, His Grace is unlikely to favour her either...His Lordship even less so. You shall not have to see her for much longer."

"I suppose you are right." She fiddled with her gloves. "Perhaps I only wish I did not have to sit down for this wretched meal with her tonight – alone! God give me strength not to lose control and wring her neck halfway through dinner!"

The younger girl giggled, making the finishing touches to the braid by pinning golden flowers with blue petals into her hair. "From the way you have described her to me, my lady, I imagine I would hardly fault you if you did wrangle her to death."

"She thinks so highly of herself – and she is by no means nearly as wise as how she perceives herself to be," she complained. "Duke Westchester is a very nice man, and I comprehend fully why Father is fond of him...what I do not understand his how he could have birthed such a wretched child. Perhaps Georgeanne Arden is the reason for Victoria's horrid nature – as Duke Westchester told my father, she claimed to fall terribly sick just this morning. It sounds an awful lot like an excuse not to go to Wellington House, if you ask me."

Penny winced. "Perhaps. Bear with it, my lady, it shall be over soon."

"Thank you for your consolation, Penelope," Emmeline sighed, smoothing out imaginary creases on the skirt of her royal blue gown. "May the Lord give me strength."

"I'm certain He will," she replied with a laugh.

The princess walked, shoulders back and left hand in her right resting on her abdomen, to one of the drawing rooms, where she found Lady Victoria scrutinising a painting with her back to the door. She noticed that it was an oil painting of the King and Queen. What were Victoria's motives? Did she lust after money? Fame? Or did she want a closer connection to the crown?

Regardless of what they were, Emmeline would find out tonight.

She cleared her throat. At the sound, Victoria turned around and curtsied, looking respectful enough even though she did not sink very low. "Good evening, Your Royal Highness."

"Lady Victoria," she greeted icily.

The Westchester drew herself back into a standing position.

"Has the palace staff been satisfactory?" Emmeline did not motion for her to sit, and both women remained standing stiffly on opposite sides of the small room.

"Of course," she replied courteously. After Emmeline's sharp questioning at lunch, it was clear that she had finally elected to show some humility – and it pleased her prospective sister-in-law to know it. The chit had shown such blatant disregard for Emmeline's father, been rude to her aunt, and had even suggested that she, a member of the royal family, had a duty to greet her in the middle of winter. She needed to be taught a lesson in respect – or many.

"Good," Emmeline responded, but her hospitality held no sign of warmth. "Sit, Lady Victoria. The appetisers are ready."

She cast her eyes over her shoulder so that they almost met the manservant behind her, and with what seemed like telepathy he instantly stepped forward to pull out her chair. She seated herself, and without a word about how her chair should also be pulled out for her her guest did the same, sliding into her seat opposite Emmeline.

The manservant bowed his broad form slightly to speak softly to his princess. "Your Highness, shall I send for the appetisers to be served?"

She nodded without meeting his eyes. "Yes, thank you."

He retreated from the room, and she looked up to smile at Victoria. The amiable gesture did not touch her eyes, which instead stayed as cold as stone. "So," she began, "do you wish to be wed to my brother?"

"Well—Well, Your Highness," she stammered, beyond shocked by the princess's directness. "I... I think it a possibility for me."

"A possibility, you say?" Immediately, Emmeline's face crumpled into a displeased frown, her eyes narrowing into daggers that cut straight into the Westchester girl's soul. "A possibility for you? I'm afraid that is an unsatisfactory response. My brother is a human being – not a object to be manipulated or an avenue to a particular way of life."

"Of...of course, Your Highness. His Lordship seems to be a wonderful man."

"That he is, Lady Victoria," was the clipped reply. "You must know that Earl Portsmouth is the finest one I have ever known. He has a heart and a soul that will make any woman he loves very happy indeed – and therefore my question for you is this. Are you of the opinion that you would be able to do the same for him?"

"I am a very qualified lady," she answered.

"I harbour no doubt for your ability to fulfil the duties of a wife, but, unfortunately, that does not qualify you to marry a man such as him." The princess straightened in her chair. "Tell me, Lady Victoria, from the bottom of your heart, do you care for my brother?"

She froze, unable to answer the question. Emerald green eyes simply stared at her, neither piercing nor curious, awaiting an answer but bearing no enquiry – all Emmeline needed now was a confirmation, a confession to intent to commit a crime all too commonplace in their society – a crime punishable by lifetimes of misery for the two people most heavily involved.

A crime Emmeline herself fallen victim to – a crime she would never allow her brother's life to be destroyed by.

The tension hanging in the air could be cut with a knife, but all it took was the kitchen girl's squeak to dispel it. "Your Royal Highness?"

"Are the appetisers ready?" she cast her eyes to the wall to her left instead as she moved to a different conversation, not directly looking at the maid as her nightmarish childhood governess Miss Paltrow had once instructed her not to when addressing servants in the presence of other nobility. Perhaps it is not an explicit rule in society, Lady Emmeline, but this is how you make yourself look more dignified, the prudish lady had once advised. Use it to display your authority. And while Emmeline usually did prefer to look directly at her servants – and treat them with a decent amount of respect – she found that Miss Paltrow had been right.

"Yes, Your Highness, I have them here."

"Serve them, if you will."

The servant had never heard the princess's voice so sharp. Though the lass was rather new to the palace and had never encountered her before, she had heard plenty about Emmeline Lockhart – the raven-haired lady with warm emerald eyes, a kind smile, an easy manner, a healthy respect for other human beings and a face that was not intimidatingly pretty.

"Yes, Princess."

The slip of a girl scurried forth to gently place the exquisite salads on the table, one plate before each diner. She then proceeded to bob a terrified curtsy and retreat to the safety of the kitchens, where no nobility ever set foot.

"Well?" Emmeline demanded once the door shut behind the maid. "Do you care for Emmett, Lady Victoria?"

The Westchester beauty swallowed. "I...I certainly hope that we might be wed."

"That does not answer my question," the princess said coldly, "but I think you have told me all I need to know – far sooner than I had expected you would. But thank you for your time, Lady Victoria, and enjoy your meal. I arranged for it to be the palace chefs' most impressive ones yet."

She stood from her chair, her crown resting steady on her jet black hair, and offered a curt nod as her last pleasantry to this snobbish girl who would likely never in her life understand the concept of love. Then she glided out of the room with as much composure and grace as she had carried herself with when she had entered.

When she exited, Penelope was standing outside the room, ready to greet her. "My lady. The kitchen girl who brought the appetisers advised me to await you here – she seemed quite shaken, too," she explained, then, with a sympathetic smile, "I take it the meal did not go well?"

"No, no, Penelope," with a light smile gracing her ruby lips, Emmeline made her reply in a carefree voice that indicated that her mood was not at all marred by the disastrous dinner. "On the contrary, it went splendidly. I have had nothing at all to eat, however – so please instruct the wait staff to bring my meal to my quarters."

"Very well, my lady," she answered, and together they proceeded down the hall.

Not long after the end of that conversation, Lady Victoria Arden was seen by the palace guard running out of the castle and leaping into a carriage, indignant tears streaming down her face.

***

HER GRACE THE DUCHESS GEORGEANNE ARDEN OF WESTCHESTER WAS most alarmed to see her oldest – and most treasured – daughter enter the house with reddened, puffy eyes and tear stains forming two streaks on her cheeks.

"My darling! What has upset you so? I enquired about Earl Portsmouth when your Papa returned some hours ago, but he only sighed at me," she exclaimed anxiously, leaping her feet when the girl came into the drawing room. "And now you come home crying!"

"Well, Mama, Emmett Lockhart seems like a very fine man, although he did not say much at dinner. He only told us that he is very busy with his duties, and that he likes to read...but he is handsome like Papa promised – devastatingly so," Victoria answered, "but his sister! Oh, she has humiliated me so!"

Her mother was wide-eyed with curiosity. "His sister, you say? The princess?"

"Yes, that wretched Princess Emmeline – oh, I despise her, Mama! She humiliated me at lunch, and then at dinner was so rude to me – she asked if I cared for her brother, and when I could not tell her that I did, she simply abandoned me and walked away!" she wailed. "She is so very arrogant, and not pretty at all, Mama, I absolutely fail to understand how she married into royalty!"

Lady Georgeanne's lips twisted into a frown, and she patted her daughter's hand reassuringly. "No matter, my darling. You have a long line of suitors – your papa only favoured this match because Earl Portsmouth is that eccentric man Duke Mayfair's son, but if Princess Emmeline truly is so terrible, he will not pursue it."

"Well, then I shall never wish to hear of the Lockharts again," she huffed. Then, with a sigh, "I am exhausted, Mama. May I retire to my quarters?"

"Yes, Victoria, of course," she replied, smiling lovingly. "Rest well, my darling."

The girl curtsied to her mother before retreating from the room, her maids in waiting already having appeared – seemingly out of thin air – and following to assist her.

***

# Chapter Six

- - - - - - - - - - - - - - - - - - - - - - - - - - - - - - - - - - - - - - - -

A/N OMG – here's the update! I'm so sorry it's late! I'm on vacation and I've completely lost my sense of time. I actually thought that today was Friday – but here it is now! Sorry, sorry, sorry!

THE DAY AFTER LADY VICTORIA'S HARRIED DEPARTURE FROM ST JAMES' Palace, the Lockhart clan gathered once more in Wellington House to discuss her performance – and their opinions on it.

"I found her wonderfully polite when she first arrived, but it did not take long for her arrogance to show," Bethany announced. "I do not approve of this match."

"You know, I will agree with your aunt," William said. "Her manner did not please me an ounce, for she was terribly rude to everyone the whole time...perhaps other than Emmett, whom she seemed keen to impress."

"I did not enjoy her complacency very much either," Emmeline agreed, frowning at the thought of it. "I shall never be able to call her Sister. I find her conceited nature so very distasteful, and when I asked her at dinner, she revealed that she did not care for Emmett at all – all she could say to me was that she would like to be married to him." Turning her attentions to her brother, she placed a gentle hand over her his clenched fist. "Emmett, you cannot marry a woman who does not care for you. You will be miserable."

Saying nothing, he drew his hand out from under hers and turned his face away from her urging gaze. She noticed his brow crumple, and her own eyebrows furrowed in response.

"Whatever is the matter? You shall not marry her. Is that not what you want?"

"I...I..." He leaned back in his chair and ran a frustrated hand over his face. "I think..."—a sigh—"I think, Emmeline, I will marry her."

"What?!" the other three in the room exclaimed simultaneously, none believing their own ears. The earl said nothing to this, only closing his eyes with a heavy exhale in utter exhaustion, and a series of indignant protests ensued:

"But she acted so rudely, nephew!"

"Did you not say that you do not wish to marry?"

"She is nothing less than absolutely horrible – you cannot marry that woman!"

"You don't understand," was all he said in return, swallowing thickly. His swept his gaze over the three horrified faces in the room and sighed again. He could not explain his intentions to them – they were very simple, and he knew exactly how to put his feelings into words, but he also knew that these words would never be accepted by his family. He was all too aware of the fact that they cared for him – they cared for him so much, too much, and they would never allow him to go through with marrying a woman for the sole purpose of tormenting himself for the rest of his life. He regretted that he had been unable to think for his sister as she would think for him. He regretted putting his happiness in front of hers – he regretted ever writing to Aunt Bethany seeking a match when his first action should have been composing a letter to his best friend proposing a match, promising a wife filled with nothing but sincerity, devotion and good intentions.

Yet instead he had let Queen Sarah court her on behalf of his son. He had said nothing when Emmeline had pleaded with him to get her out of the arrangement. Because of his inaction there was now a crown resting on her head, on her shoulders, on her spirit, a duty to another man and an entire kingdom that stated that she would never in her life find the bliss and happiness she deserved. Emmett of all people knew best how she deserved happiness...she had shown the purest parts of her soul to him, her grin, her delicious hand-baked blueberry pie, and her ardent passion for the violoncello. He should have been the first person to fight for her happiness – and he had been the very last. In fact, he had hardly fought for her at all, only watched as his father duelled the King for Emmeline and almost gave his life because of it. Then he had watched as Emmeline gave her life away to save William's.

Was it not, in this context, only right that he should marry a woman as horrible as Lady Victoria Arden? If his sister could not be happy in marriage, why should he ever be? Giving away his chance at love to solidify ties between Mayfair and Westchester and, more importantly, to fulfil his father's wishes that his son might marry his dear friend's daughter seemed only a just way to punish himself...

"Explain this to me, Emmett," Emmeline demanded flatly. "Tell me why you would do this to yourself – to us – to me."

"There is nothing to be explained," he replied. "It...it is an advantageous match. I have a duty to the Lockhart family—"

Her eyes narrowed immediately, and he knew she had already seen through his lies. After all, no one in the world knew him better than she. "A duty, you say? Tell me then, Emmett, when did you begin to believe in – what did you call it? – oh, yes, marriage and heirs?"

"I do not," he snapped, frustrated – albeit with no one but himself. "I—I care for Lady Victoria!"

"Oh, come now, brother, do not insult yourself so. Do not insult me so! Do you really think I would believe this? I have known you all my life, and I have known you better every day. Do you really believe that I, your twin sister, would believe that you, the most free-spirited lover of life in my acquaintance, care for that conceited, superficial, two-faced, power-hungry wretch?" Emmeline was close to shouting now, and with every word she spoke her eyebrows drew closer and closer to the bridge of her nose.

"Do not speak of Victoria thusly, Emmeline, I told you I—"

"I will speak of her however I please, Emmett, Victoria Arden is nothing but a repulsive woman trying to get ahold of your power and your money and you shall never marry her!" she roared, finally driven to outright rage. She stood from her seat. "As for you – you are being an absolute idiot, and I will not speak to you until you have decided to be otherwise!"

She huffed, turned, and stormed out of the library, leaving her father and aunt staring after her in pure shock and her brother feeling more dejected than he had in days. The door slammed behind her, the sound echoing for the longest few seconds Emmett Lockhart had ever experienced. Not long after, her carriage left Wellington House, bound for the palace; where she would run up the courtyard steps, fling herself into her room, hold her pillow and cry for hours.

Emmeline simply did not understand why her brother would not see sense.

***

EARL PORTSMOUTH DID NOT HEAR FROM HER ROYAL HIGHNESS THE princess for many days after that. He did not seek her out, nor did she take any initiative to speak to him, and both siblings found themselves rather miserable. Of course, this was a battle of two equally stubborn wills, and neither would ever admit how much they missed the other.

Emmett had since written to Lady Victoria asking for permission to call on her. He did not hear back from her, and on a particularly cloudy day, he had decided to visit the Ardens' London residence despite the lack of an affirmative reply. He would ask for her hand in marriage, and then he would marry her, and he would finally feel some of his guilt laid to rest.

At least, that was how it was all meant to work.

Sometime in the afternoon, his carriage arrived in their driveway, rolling smoothly over the cobblestone. A footman greeted him the moment he stepped out of it, directing him to wait in the drawing room while he sought out members of the family to receive him.

While he awaited the duke, duchess, or their daughter, Emmett found himself examining the portraits on the walls. There were paintings of ancestors, stately gentlemen and ravishing women, as well as more familiar faces hanging on the walls, including a family portrait of the jolly Duke Westchester, a very pretty younger Lady Victoria, and a beautiful woman who must have been her mother the Duchess Georgeanne. Much like Victoria, she had hair a rich shade of chocolate and eyes the same hue. Emmett had never witnessed beauty such as hers except in his own mother, and he understood where the bride he sought had inherited her outward appearance from.

Perhaps she had found her inward appearance from her mother also, for as Emmett had observed, the most beautiful people tended to be the most snobbish. Years of being fawned over and praise had the tendency to give individuals a false sense of entitlement...

"Ah, Earl Portsmouth." A woman's pinched voice interrupted his rumination, and he turned to face the older woman whose image he had just been gazing upon. Indeed, she had brown hair and eyes, though they were far more luxurious than what the artist had been able to capture. She was wrapped in an exquisite satin dress, a shawl draped over her shoulders to protect her from the winter. Duchess Georgeanne smiled almost flirtatiously at him, although both knew that her husband was his father's dear friend and he sought her daughter's hand in marriage. Nonetheless, Emmett dared not read too much into the arch of her eyebrows and the slight pout of her lips, only bowing respectfully to her.

"Good afternoon, Your Grace."

"Good afternoon," she echoed, a shadow of a smile lingering on her lips. He could hardly tell if she was smiling or if it was only a trick of the light. "I apologise – my husband is not in the house today, and therefore I greet you on his behalf. Whatever brings you to our humble residence, Your Lordship?"

"I did write to your daughter Lady Victoria, Madam, asking if I could call on her," he replied. "Unfortunately, I did not receive a response. I was, however, hoping to see her anyway..."

"I see," she said, a slight pout coming onto her lips. She paused, then gestured to one of the plush chairs in the room. "Have a seat, Sir."

Bowing slightly by way of thanks, Emmett complied. The duchess seated herself opposite him and, once they were both settled, said, "My daughter spoke highly of you."

A smile came upon his face. "Oh, I—"

"But," she interrupted piercingly, her entire expression morphing into something more sharp than seductive and the allure of her brown eyes vanishing as they turned shrewd, "your sister will prove to be a challenge if this match is to be made. Poor Victoria came home crying the night of her dinner with Her Highness because she had been humiliated so unfairly. She does not wish to hear of you or your family ever again."

Emmett opened his mouth to say something, but did not know what he could offer in reply. Duchess Georgeanne seemed to notice this, for her chin tilted upward immediately. "Unless you are able to persuade Her Highness to better her attitude toward my daughter and offer a public apology, I'm afraid I could never approve of this match. If you do succeed in doing so, however...you will have my utmost support. I will advise my daughter to do what is best for her, and coupled with my husband's wish for the pair of you to be married, we shall hold the wedding ceremony very soon."

She smiled at him, and perhaps she had meant for it to look pleasant, but there was something about the action that quite reminded Emmett of a fox.

"Your Grace...I am thankful for your help, but my sister – she is not one to apologise for something she does not think is right."

"And that is your problem, not mine." Duchess Georgeanne's smile did not falter. "Besides, if Her Highness thinks that making an innocent young lady cry is the right thing to do, perhaps her moral compass requires recalibration, yes?"

He felt a pang of rage surge in his heart at this blatant accusation against his sister's heart – which he was certain was made of naught but pure gold

–, but hastily quieted it, instead offering a slight smile to the catty woman. "I will speak to her, Your Grace."

"Very good," she purred, her satisfaction with his concession obvious. She stood, and he was quick to follow. Their conversation was over.

She flashed him a saccharine smile. "My footman will show you out. Good day to you, Your Lordship."

Then she was gone, but a silhouette of satin and cashmere, and he was left standing alone wondering how on earth he would persuade Emmeline Lockhart, the Princess of the land and the most spirited lass he knew, to offer a public apology.

***

# Chapter Seven

"MY LADY?" PENELOPE POKED HER HEAD INTO PRINCESS EMMELINE'S quarters. "I know you wish to be alone, my lady, but Her Majesty has invited you to dine with the rest of the family in the hall." She paused. "Besides, dining with the rest of the family would be good for you...talking with Her Majesty instead of staying here by yourself."

"Very well, then," she replied with an inaudible sigh and a resigned smile. "Walk with me?"

"Of course, my lady," was the obliging response. Emmeline drew herself to her feet and Penny escorted her to to the dining hall, where the other members of the royal family were already seated – all of them.

Not just King Andrew, Queen Sarah, and Crown Prince Alexander – but all six of them, the previously small unit of three joined by Their Royal Highnesses the Princes Frederick, Javier and Lionel.

When had they returned?

Emmeline was by no means prepared for their arrival!

She knew nothing of them, but that they had all been sent abroad to different parts of the empire, including the colonies, to travel all of the land and the sea belonging to the Crown. They were to meet their subjects with the goal of inspiring patriotism everywhere, and had left the palace approximately three years ago. The oldest brother stayed – the Queen had more important designs for him, designs Emmeline had since become a part of. She remembered how there had been great excitement in all parts of the land when the plans of the princes' tour had been announced, and she herself had met with the youngest brother Lionel when he had visited Portsmouth only two years before. The Queen had mentioned her sons in passing before, but she had not gone into detail nor had she mentioned their imminent return to London, and Emmeline found herself rooted to the spot in pure shock at their sudden appearance. Her head began to spin.

Penelope, who had also gone rigid beside her, looked equally taken aback.

"Oh!" Queen Sarah exclaimed when she saw her daughter-in-law standing at the entrance and looking quite distraught. "Come quickly, my dearest, we have all been waiting for you. I apologise if this has caught you off-guard; I did forget to mention that the rest of my children were due to return to the castle today."

Emmeline fainted promptly.

***

"...WILL SHE BE ALL RIGHT, ALEXANDER?"

Emmeline woke to the sound of a man's concerned whisper.

"I imagine so." Her husband's voice reached her ears next. "I spoke with her lady-in-waiting. She seems to be in the habit of swooning when she is taken by surprise."

"In the habit, you say? You make it sound like a choice."

"Well, Freddy, you know they say that one never knows how it is with women. Emmeline thus far has been quite tolerable, but I hear that some women are terribly strange creatures."

"I will assure you that fainting is most definitely not a choice, Alexander, and women would not be so strange if men were only kinder to their hearts." Her voice came out dry and weak, and when she forced her eyes open her vision was blurry. Immediately the two male figures rushed to her bedside, and upon closer inspection she saw that the man standing beside her husband, whose voice she knew, was the second brother Frederick. He resembled Alexander strikingly, with the same fawn-coloured hair and clear blue eyes, tall nose and distinct jawline, although she noticed that his face lacked the brooding air her husband's always carried with him. Of course, now that the wedding was over and done with, Alexander looked less troubled on a daily basis, but smiles still came rarely – if at all – to his face. There seemed to be a shadow always lingering over his countenance. His brother, however, looked far more happy and youthful, far more likely to laugh, if she could so judge a person by only one glance at his face. Did that make him more handsome?—Perhaps, for Emmeline did always like a man who smiled.

"I apologise, Emmeline, I imagine falling unconscious is hardly pleasant." Alexander interrupted her inward analysis of their faces. His voice held no sign of teasing, and something moved in her chest at the sound of genuine worry. "Can I help you with anything?—Water, perhaps?"

"Yes," she replied, her voice hoarse, "water, if you would be so kind."

"I will fetch a glass at once." He was out of the room before she could blink, leaving her alone with Prince Frederick. Silence hung over them, neither knowing what to say to the other.

"I do apologise for missing your wedding," he finally said, breaking the quiet. "I hear it was lovely."

"And I apologise for fainting before I could even curtsy to you," she answered with a tired chuckle.

"Well, I suppose I must then apologise for coming completely unannounced," he responded with a wry smile. He pulled a chair from under her vanity and sat down a respectable distance away from her. "I am sorry that we frightened you, you know. I assure you we had no intention to do so – Mother was supposed to tell you that we were coming home."

Emmeline smiled resignedly and shook her head. "It is no matter. I am quite all right now." She paused, realising that neither knew how to address the other, both only clear on the fact that they were now of equal status. "Since we are family, you – and the rest of your brothers – may simply call me Emmeline, as Alexander does."

"And you may call us by our given names," he said. "Mine is Frederick."

"You know, all the people of the kingdom already have your names and faces committed to memory," she said with a teasing lilt to her voice and her smile stretching wider into the likes of a grin, "and I am most certainly not new here. I require no introduction from any of you."

"Of course." Frederick's face turned a shade pinker with embarrassment.

Emmeline laughed, but then noticed how dry her mouth was becoming and remarked, "I really am quite thirsty now. I hope Alexander returns soon."

"Shall I go to find him, Sister?"

"No need," she said. "I'm sure he will not take much longer."

He did not; when he returned, hasty and on the brink of breaking into perspiration, it was revealed that he had been been waylaid by Queen Sarah on his way to find a glass of water, who was very worried for her daughter-in-law's wellbeing. He had then hurried all the way back, not wanting to deprive Emmeline of her water any longer. He showered her with apologies before handing her the glass, and she smiled his concern away before drinking gratefully.

Frederick watched this exchange with a curious eye. He had heard things, many things, about their union – it had not been a willing one, he knew, and he had even heard a rumour about a duel between their fathers over it...then there was word of a handsome navy man and Emmeline's broken heart – but none of it showed now, and he wondered about all the dramatic things he had heard and felt a sense of pride swell in his chest as he looked upon his typically less attentive older brother, the ever-rebellious Crown Prince Alexander, who now watched the raven-haired girl with naught but warmth in his blue eyes.

"I will excuse myself now," Frederick finally announced. "You must want some time alone with your wife, Alex."

Emmeline waited for him to say that they needed no time alone, to invite him to stay with them, but instead her husband nodded at his brother with a ghost of a smile upon his lips. "Thank you, Freddy."

The second St James son bowed to his sister-in-law, she smiled at him, and he left the room.

Alexander turned to her once more. "How are you feeling, Emmeline?"

"I feel well enough," she replied with an easy laugh. His concern only seemed to tickle her. "I was only surprised, Alexander, not ill."

"You must notify me if you should feel unwell at any point in time," he urged. "Promise me that you will."

"Very well," she said with a melodramatic sigh and a teasing glint in her emerald eyes. "I promise you."

Although she had made the requested vow, he did not seem reassured. He cast his eyes away from her and swallowed, his eyebrows creasing slightly as he did so. At this sight the mischief in her eyes vanished, she and beheld her husband with a slight frown. When they had first met, he had been so rude to her. After their wedding, he had adopted a clipped civility with her. But never had he shown so much concern for her, a girl she assumed he did not care a jot for. She supposed to be nobody to him.

"Alexander?" she said quietly, almost timid as she looked upon the man she whose intentions towards her she had thought were crystal clear.

"Yes?" he returned his gaze to her, but he did not seem relieved of his worry.

"Why... What is all this?"

"I don't understand what you mean."

"I—" Confused beyond belief, she shut her eyes and held her face in her left hand, exhaling heavily. When she finally raised her head to speak again, she said, "I simply thought you did not care for me."

He said nothing for a long while, and Emmeline expected him to realise that he in truth did not. She expected him to stand and leave, walk away as he always did from her, leaving behind nothing but a polite silence, a coldness perhaps better than his hot temper but far worse than anything she had ever imagined her married life would be like. She expected him to go and leave her thinking of her Peter, the man who would never have left her alone, the man who would have held her and told her that he loved her, the man whom she loved, the man who cared for her.

He did not.

"How could I not care for you?" was the reply that made her heart stop. "You are intelligent and kind and genuine, and most of all, Emmeline, you are my wife. I do not love you as you deserve to be loved, and for that I am more sorry than you could ever imagine...but you have come to be one of the people I hold dearest. We will be partners all our lives, and I hope to be there with you, for you. I...I cannot love you the way you must yearn to be loved, but I would very much like to love you in whatever way I can."

"I..."

Something caught in Emmeline's throat, and a runaway tear fled from her eyelid and ran down her cheek. She fought to hold her emotions in, but the resistance proved to be futile, and before she could apologise for it she was sobbing into her hands. Startled, Alexander hurriedly moved to draw her into his arms, running his hand up and down over her back in consolation, trying to stop it all.

"Have I said something wrong? I apologise for upsetting you, Emmeline, please do not cry so..."

He would never want to be the man to make her cry – when he had decided this he did not know, but over days of seeing her only at dinnertime, weeks of exchanging courteous words with her, and months of realising that she was in just much pain as he was, he had finally chosen to open his heart to Emmeline, only hoping that hers would not be locked away from him. Her last name was, after all, Lockhart.

Fortunately for him, she was a girl with an open heart.

"No," she said, pulling away from him to meet his gaze and laugh through her tears to assure him that she was quite fine, "no, Alexander. You have said everything right."

***

A/N TGIF EVERYONE!! I really really loved writing this chapter – there was so much emotion and Emmeline's life is finally settling down a little :) I hope you enjoyed reading it just as much!

Also, am I the only one who kinda thinks that Alex and Emmeline are cute together??

Let me know what you think! Till next time! :)

# Chapter Eight

----------------------------------------------------------------

**W**hen I fell down you'd be there holding me up. Spread your wings as you go; when God takes you back He'll say "Hallelujah, you're home."

EMMETT LOCKHART'S FOOTSTEPS ECHOED THE HEAVI-NESS OF HIS HEART as he trudged through the hallway towards his sister's study. He could hear them ricocheting in the empty hallway, along with the pounding of his pulse in his ears. He had never felt so anxious on his way to meet his sister – she had, in fact, always calmed him when he was most nervous. Her eyes were adoring and kind, her smile the most genuine he had ever seen, and her embrace was always able to quiet the storms that raged in his oft-troubled soul. She was his oasis, a safe, quiet harbour he always came back to after voyaging the turbulent seas. She was the one person whom he had always loved, and who had always loved him. They had had each other since birth, each serving as a constant pillar of support for the other, a source of motivation, a reason to live and to live well...

But this time was different. He was not here to seek her consolation. He needed this meeting to go well. He swallowed the lump in his throat, each step becoming harder to take as he neared the study.

Perhaps, somewhere in the back of his mind, he already knew that his words would cut her heart.

A passing maid bowed to him but the weight on his mind meant that he did not see her, green eyes fixed on the narrow path in front of him.

Emmeline, I'm sorry, he rehearsed inwardly for the fifty-first time that day. I would never hurt you on purpose, but I have to marry her. I cannot explain it to you...it is just something that must be done. Please, for me... apologise to Lady Victoria. She will not have me otherwise. Clenching and unclenching his fists once, he inhaled deeply to steady his erratic heartbeat and his rocking gut.

Finally, he arrived at the door which had come to be familiar to him. Closing his eyes, he took another shaky calming breath. He raised his fist and hesitated for brief moment before rapping on the hardwood.

"Come in." Her voice was loud and clear, but it held none of her usual cheer.

Emmett pushed the door open. She lifted her gaze from the book before her, and stiffened immediately as their eyes met. Ramrod straight, she closed the collection of poems slowly, slid it to one side of the table, and spoke.

"How can I help you, Earl Portsmouth?"

"Emmeline, I'm sorry," he said. "I would never hurt you on purpose, but I have to marry her. I—"

"You are not sorry," she interrupted, her voice steady and quiet but sharp as a blade plunging into his soul. "If you were, you would not be saying such preposterous things. You are your own person with your own life that you have every right to make as happy as you can – you do not have to marry her, Emmett. She does not own your soul, and...and neither do I."

Just because I am unhappy does not mean you have to be as well, she meant to say. Her brother, however, heard something very different.

"If you do not own my soul, you should respect my right to make my own choices. I know you think you are doing what is best for me, Emmeline, but I am able to choose my own bride."

Her eyebrows furrowed, and she felt her throat start to close. His obstinacy broke her heart.

Still she managed a response. "Do you, really?"

She closed her eyes briefly and, trembling, sucked in a breath of air. Then her green eyes were dry and cold, and she said with all the curtness of an offended lady, "If you have no other business here, Earl Portsmouth, you are excused."

She picked her book up once more, swallowed the tears that threatened to fall, and pretended to read. He looked upon her and saw her heartbreak, but he could not leave now.

"I do have other business, Emmeline," he replied. "I need a favour from you."

She ignored him, instead running her eyes over the same lines over and over again and praying he would give up and quit the room so that she could cry her angry tears without being seen. She did not want him to see her weep for him, for she hated him – in that moment, she hated him with every fibre in her body. He was acting like an idiot, and she loved him so dearly that seeing him behaving so ignited not just ache in her heart but a raging fire in her stomach. She would not let him ruin himself – as long as she breathed, he would not let his stupidity get the better of him.

And so her gaze remained stubbornly affixed on her book, her fist clenched under the table as she willed her eyes to stay dry.

"I need you to apologise to Lady Victoria," he said, watching her carefully as her shaking became more and more obvious with every word he spoke. "Her mother demanded a public apolo—"

"No!"

Within a split second, her ire erupted like a volcano, and she stood from her chair with such speed and force that she toppled it behind her. She slammed her book shut and stalked over to him, the vein in her temple throbbing.

"Get out of my study. Leave the palace!" she shouted, laying her hands on his chest to push him out the door. Ultimately, however, he was much stronger than her, and did not take a single step back. She shoved harder and still he refused to budge.

"Guards!" she cried. "Guards!"

He stood staring at her as two palace guards rushed into the room and she ordered them to see him out of the premises. They were about to seize him when he turned sharply away, nimbly avoiding their rough grasp.

"Please consider it, Emmeline. I...I need your help."

Then, voluntarily, he left the room. The guards followed to ensure that he would quit the palace altogether, and when the door closed behind them, Emmeline let out a shaky breath.

Before, she would never have thrown her him out.

Tears streamed down her cheeks.

Emmett Lockhart, her own brother, her closest ally and best friend – she would never have chased him away from her.

She cradled her face in her hands, and her shoulders began to shake gently.

But he was not acting like her brother would have. Victoria Arden was everything he should have despised.

A whimper.

Despite a lack of confirmation from him, she was certain that he was on some rash, misguided and completely illogical quest to redeem himself after all that had happened with her marriage…

She let out a strangled sob.

His heart was set on securing this union doomed to a lifetime of misery, and he the only person Emmeline knew to be as strong-headed as herself. It had always been this way: if he did not give in to her first solely out of his affections, their battle of wills would be a never-ending one. How could she possibly talk him out of this asinine endeavour before the deed was done?

She cried harder yet. She could not bear to see another tragedy come unto the Lockhart family – it would smash the fragments of her already-broken heart.

Were two loveless marriages not yet enough for that foolish boy?

***

QUEEN SARAH'S DELIGHT WAS CLEAR AS SHE GUSHED ON AND ON ABOUT her wonderful plans for her sons' welcome back to the capital, but Emmeline could not bring herself to smile obediently like she normally would – poking dully at her pig roast with her mind full of her brother's affairs, she could hardly force herself to pay attention to what her mother-in-law was saying.

"...and I have had an order placed for a hundred dozen yellow roses," she concluded animatedly. "I have never seen a party with so many flowers. A hundred dozen – will that not be beautiful, my dear?"

"I am certain that it shall be like no other, beloved," King Andrew replied patiently, a faint smile upon his face. "Your welcome party shall be wonderful. Are you not pleased, children? You are blessed to have such a loving mother, are you not?"

"Extremely," Frederick answered obligingly, grinning broadly at both his parents. "Thank you, Mother. I'm sure I speak for all three of us when I say that we look forward to the ball immensely."

Sarah laughed. "Thank you both, but I was in sooth addressing Emmeline."

"Oh!" Emmeline yelped at the sound of her name. "Er—yes, Sarah. Absolutely stunning."

The Queen seemed unconvinced, but made no further comment, instead saying: "The party will be held in a month. I am sorry it could not be sooner, children, but it would take quite some time for all the invitations to be sent to every lord and lady in the land. Besides, you all shall need new suits to look presentable, and Emmeline and I new dresses. I imagine the tailor will also require a fair amount of time to achieve perfection, and we will settle for no less..."

***

AFTER HE HAD LEFT HIS SISTER CRYING ALONE IN HER STUDY, EMMETT Lockhart returned to Wellington House to write, once again, to Lady Victoria Arden, begging her for her audience. With his letter he sent her a bouquet of fine red roses.

A week went by and he began to suspect that she would not give in to him – not, at least, until he had fulfilled her mother's demand.

Not letting her silence discourage him, he sent her, next, another letter ridden with honey-sweet words and accompanied by a silver necklace.

He knew her type – the type of woman whose hand could be bought with money and power, the type of woman who claimed to be in possession of better morals than a whore but hardly was. He was determined that he would win this woman's affections. All he needed to do was shower her with pricey gifts to prove his affluence, and she would sooner or later change her mind. He was one of the most desired bachelors across the kingdom, and he was certain that Lady Victoria just needed to be reminded of this.

Two weeks into his relentless pursuit of her, he was prepared to send her another love letter with a gold hairpin, and the two items sat neatly on his desk.

"Your Lordship?" There was a rap on the door. "The mail has arrived."

"Thank you, Collins. Is there anything at all from Lady Victoria Arden?"

"I'm afraid not, Sir." The footman stepped up to stand by him at his desk, handing him a handful of envelopes. "One invitation from the palace, and some correspondence from Portsmouth."

"Very well." In return, he gave Collins the hairpin and letter. "Have this sent to the Arden estate for me, will you?"

"Of course, Sir."

Emmett nodded to dismiss him, and when he was alone in his study, he let out a heavy sigh. If spending all this money will win Victoria Arden's favour, I suppose it is worth it, he thought to himself. I do wonder, however, how much keeping her heart would cost me. My entire fortune, perhaps, and Father's too.

He chuckled defeatedly at this thought before turning his attentions instead to the correspondence he had received. Two letters from some merchants in Portsmouth...and a golden envelope from St James' Palace.

It promised a ball with dancing and music to welcome home Their Royal Highnesses the Princes Frederick, Javier and Lionel of England and requested his presence at the celebration.

Between the lines, however, Emmett read something more: a chance to see Lady Victoria Arden, and a second opportunity to meet with sister.

***

A/N Thank you for reading. As always, do feel free to and comment. Till next week.

# Chapter Nine

-----------------------------------------------------------------

A/N Eep—hey everyone! I'm so sorry that this is so late!! Either way, I hope you enjoy whatever's left with the weekend with this chapter of Apollo!

EMMELINE'S TROUBLED EXPRESSION HAD NOT LEFT HER FACE FOR DAYS now. Alexander had asked about it several times in private, but she had only shaken her head softly and offered a sad smile with an unconvincing promise that she was just fine. Queen Sarah, on the other hand, had also noticed her uncharacteristic gloom, but had elected not to make enquiries until her daughter-in-law was ready to speak of it on her own accord.

On one Wednesday afternoon, however, she could take it no longer, and, with a frown upon her face, finally asked, "Is something the matter, dearest? You know you can tell us if anything at all is wrong."

"Oh, no, nothing is wrong," she lied, mustering a half-hearted smile as an attempt at providing some kind of evidence. "You—You must be mistaken, Sarah. I... I am only tired – there is nothing else. I apologise if it seemed otherwise."

But Queen Sarah saw through this immediately, and a sceptical raise of the monarch's eyebrows was all it took for the truth to come tumbling out of her mouth.

"It's my brother," she confessed. "He has his heart set on marrying this atrocious woman – Lady Victoria Arden of Westchester. She is the most terrible creature I have ever met: she is rude, she is arrogant, and she hungers for my brother's money and fame. She seems not to understand what love is, or value it very much at all, and thinks of her match as naught but a possibility for herself!"

"Oh, I know her kind," the queen replied with a knowing smile. "I am not quite fond of them myself."

"What should I do, Sarah?—Emmett refuses to listen," she said. "I was unkind to the lass when I met her, and now he wants me to issue a public apology so that he can win her favour again."

"Oh, dear." The older woman sighed. "Would you like me to retract the Ardens' invitation to the boys' welcome party?"

Her smile was resigned as she dismissed the offer with a gentle shake of her head. "No, no. That would probably be unwise. I do not wish to incur...unnecessary political ramifications over a family affair."

"You are being very sensible, my dear, thank you for being so considerate." Sarah paused for a brief moment, before a sly smile crept onto her face, an impish light coming into her aged eyes. "Very well, Emmeline, listen closely. This is what we will do..."

***

THE WEEKS WHIZZED BY, AND SOIRÉE PREPARATIONS SIG-
NIFIED THAT ST James' Palace, along with the rest of the capital and
the homes of the noble and royal-blooded across the land, was a flurry of
activity, every pair of hands busy making things perfect for the welcoming
home of the three princes to the capital. Maids and servants of the palace
were cleaning and decorating, and seamstresses were drowning in fabrics
as they wove dress after dress and jacket after jacket for all the partygoers
in the land. Attendees spent their time at fittings and primping themselves
for the event, all eager to put their best faces forward in the presence of
the complete noble family – now equipped with a recently throne-ready
Crown Prince and his new wife.

The Queen and her daughter-in-law were no exception. They experiment-
ed with various creams and serums, Sarah enjoying the fulfilment of having
a daughter to fuss over and Emmeline delighting in the experience of
feeling the love of a mother once again. The royal tailors had designed them
fine dresses for the evening, and they spent hours each day standing for
fittings. The five men of the palace, of course, were not spared from Sarah's
wrath, and were constantly in appointments with the tailors as well, having
new jackets, shirts and pants prepared for the ball.

The Arden girls and their mother were also busy dolling themselves up
for the party. Duchess Georgeanne spent a large amount of her husband's
fortune procuring dresses, creams and various powders for herself and her
daughters, hoping to catch, in particular, the eyes of the three newly-ar-
rived princes. They were, without a doubt, the most eligible bachelors for
her daughters to marry, and Frederick St James specifically seemed to be
a very fine man for her eldest. He was responsible, courteous, refined and
quite dashing. More importantly than all this, however, was the fact that
he was currently second in line to the throne.

In Wellington House, in the meantime, Emmett Lockhart was also ready-
ing himself for the grand party, seeing the family tailor frequently to have

new clothes made for it. His father William, however, did not seem as interested in investing in a new set of formal wear for the event, instead content to simply watch his son be a vain young man. He knew that the boy had a woman to impress that night – that snobbish Westchester lass, and though he did not approve, he had elected not to make any further comments about the match after being quite rudely refuted by the boy some days ago.

It had nearly been a fortnight before the ball when he had raised his concerns to his son. He had noticed the opulent gifts being sent to the Arden estate, and said one evening at dinner, "Emmett, do you really wish to woo Lady Victoria?"

"Of course, Father," the matter-of-fact response had been. "She would be a very advantageous choice, would she not?"

"She would," William had replied carefully, "but perhaps she would also be an unwise one."

"How so?" He already sounded disinterested at this point in the conversation, and the older man knew that his words would only fall on deaf ears.

"You would be very unhappy," he had said. "But you are already aware of this."

"I know what I am doing, Father, and I am certain that I am making the right choice. Both you and Emmeline simply need to accept that I am a grown man capable of making decisions that are advantageous to the family – no longer just an obstinate child with a point to prove." Then he had risen from the table. "I'm afraid I've lost my stomach, Father. Enjoy your meal; I will see you tomorrow."

William had only smiled resignedly and said naught more, but he knew that if his son was anything at all, he was an obstinate child with a point to prove.

***

THE EVENING OF THE SPECTACULAR WELCOME BALL HAD ARRIVED, AND the royal family was making their final preparations. The ballroom was already filled with lords and ladies, chattering livelily and enjoying the complimentary drinks and hors d'oeuvres as they awaited the entrance of the monarchs.

"I truly am sorry for dragging you into this, Alexander." Emmeline sighed as she watched her husband straighten his cravat. "It's just that that Victoria lass was so obnoxious, I needed someone to talk to...and then Sarah insisted and—"

"No, no," he replied dismissively, waving her worries away as he examined his suit in the mirror before him. "Do not fault yourself for any such thing. I know how Mother is – and, besides, if you truly do despise her thusly, the least I can do as your husband is to be there for you while you are forced to put up with the likes of her."

A sinking silence hung in the air as Emmeline made no response. She must have been thinking of her navy-man again – he could feel her heavy-heartedness as he said the word husband. Even after their emotional connection several days ago, the fact remained that her heart belonged to Peter Jamison.

Hoping to lighten the mood and brighten hers, the prince added, "Who knows? I might even slip in an insult or two."

"You will do no such thing, Alexander, you are a prince!" Emmeline exclaimed, laughing so hard she nearly fell off her perch on the arm of one of the plush chairs in his quarters.

He turned to grin at her, blue eyes twinkling with mischief. "All the more reason for me to express my disdain at her, then. After all, royals are designed to be dramatic."

"I'm afraid you might be the only one, Alexander. I have never in all my years met a royal as theatric as you." Tilting her head slightly to examine his state of dress, she decided herself dissatisfied and stood from the chair to go to him.

He let her adjust his jacket and cravat while he made his next remark. "Well, you have met my father."

"I suppose that is true," she hummed as her delicate fingers tugged gently on the fabric. She swept away imaginary creases in his shirt and patted his chest twice in quick succession to announce her happiness with her own handiwork. "You must have inherited his dramatics, then."

"Thank you," he said with a gentle smile, looking down at her braided black hair and emerald green eyes before surveying her gown for the first time that evening. His blue eyes were kindly, and they held a certain affection – the type a man would hold for a sister or a dear friend. "Have I mentioned that that is a beautiful dress?"

Emmeline smiled back at him, drawing herself away from his warmth. "No – no, you have not, Alexander, but thank you...for everything." She paused as she picked her gloves up from the chair she had claimed as hers and slid them on. "Come now. We ought to be punctual tonight."

The duo walked arm-in-arm to the ballroom, and when they entered the crier announced their presence. All in the room turned to greet them but the monarchs seated at their thrones, whom they approached. Alexander bowed and Emmeline swept into a deep curtsy, the sight of which seemed to delight Queen Sarah terribly.

"Rise – rise, children," she said, turning her head to beam at her husband. "Oh, Andrew, look at them! Are they not such a handsome pair?"

"Indeed they are, my love." He smiled lovingly at her, and the sight of it sparked a pang in Emmeline's chest, for she too used to have a man who would smile at her that way...a man who must have been in the colonies for months now, a victim of his heart's exile.

She felt a gentle weight come to fall upon the hand she had in the crook of Alexander's arm, and when she cast her eyes down at it, she saw that her husband had placed his other hand on hers. She turned to look at him, and his blue eyes locked encouragingly with her green ones, urging her to remember that she had bigger things to think of tonight. She managed to smile slightly at him, telling him with a small nod that she understood.

Then he turned his gaze back to Sarah. "Mother, where are the boys?"

"Oh – they've already gone dancing," the Queen replied. Then, with a laugh, "They seem to be quite popular with the young ladies in attendance tonight."

"I'm sure they are," he agreed with a knowing smile. "They are princes, after all. I'm sure every young woman here is hoping to catch their eye."

She laughed. "It wasn't long ago that every young lady in the land was hoping to catch yours." A pause. "All right, children, the pair of you ought to go dancing as well. If I recall correctly, Emmeline has a number of introductions to make tonight."

The black-haired girl smiled. "Indeed, Sarah."

"Off you go, then," she said.

Alexander bowed and Emmeline curtsied, and their mother nodded her acknowledgement with kind, smiling eyes. Then he offered her his arm, she took it, and they descended the steps together. They stood to face one another on the dance floor, and he asked, "May I have this dance?"

She laughed. The formal request felt foreign to them both – it felt as if he were courting her, or as if they were the husband and wife everyone thought that they were, even though Alexander had never played a romantic role in her life, as she had never been a lover to him.

Nonetheless, she nodded.

"You may."

***

# Chapter Ten

---

A /N Happy Good Friday to all Christian readers! And to all readers, here's Chapter Ten – I hope you enjoy it! As usual, votes and comments mean a lot, so do leave one behind – if you would be so kind! :)

THAT NIGHT, EMMELINE LOCKHART LEARNED HOW DIF-FERENT DANCING with a friend was from dancing with a lover, or her brother.

It was not worse or better, as one might call it – only different. When Emmett held her she was in her safe haven, and when Peter spun her around she felt like she was the only woman in the world. When she danced with Alexander St James all she could do was laugh, and she truly understood for the first time the reason why dancing was considered a social activity.

She saw her brother once or twice. He was naught but a figure in the crowd, but she would always be able to recognise him. She knew his silhouette better than she knew anyone's, and she had memorised every one of his features down to the last hair on his head. Their eyes did not meet, and he did not go to her. Alexander noticed her face fall at each sight of her brother and was always quick to divert her attention with a witty line, and before she knew it she would be smiling again.

"Shall we go to speak with that Victoria Arden?" he asked after they had danced for some time. She was engaged in conversation with a girl at one side of the ballroom, and he spied the brown-haired young lady through the crowd. "I do think I see the lass."

"I think I would like to introduce you now," Emmeline answered. A pause. "Thank you for all this, Alexander."

"For all of what?" he replied with an easy smile. "We are family, beloved. I will always stand by you – and I will let everyone know it. Whoever offends you will offend me far more."

She laughed. "Whenever did you become such a dear, beloved?"

"When I realised just how wonderful you are."

Emmeline burst out in giggles. "You must be the funniest man I know."

"What an honour. But come now." He offered her his arm. "We have a snob to intimidate."

She smiled her gratitude to him. "Yes – that we do."

And so together they approached the snooty girl, who stood chattering animatedly with her company.

He cleared his throat, and Victoria's eyes fluttered to meet his. Instantly she dropped into a flawless curtsy, her friend following hastily.

"Your Royal Highness," she greeted. "Whatever brings me the pleasure?"

"Whoever, Lady Victoria," he corrected with some edge to his tone. "We saw you in the crowd, and my wife wished to introduce us."

"Oh, yes, of course. Princess Emmeline."

"Do rise," she replied with a pleasant enough smile. When Victoria was standing at her full height once more and her friend had scampered away with one scathing glance from the snooty girl, she said, "I would like to offer something of an apology, Lady Victoria. I understand I quite rattled you the other night. I meant to make my point, not quite to cause you such immense grief."

"Well—ah—yes," she choked out. "I was...slightly upset."

Emmeline cocked her head with a slight lift of her eyebrows, her smile never leaving her lips. "Only slightly? Well, that does come as a surprise to me, given that my brother came naught but barging to my study demanding that I make a public apology to you."

"Yes," Alexander said. "I do wonder what my wife has to apologise for, Lady Victoria. Is she not entitled to her opinion that you are not compatible with my brother-in-law? Is she not entitled to be upset should someone view her brother, whom she loves dearly, as a means of gaining money and power rather than a human being?"

"Oh! That was all my mother's doing," Victoria blurted out.

The princess narrowed her eyes slightly. "I'm afraid I don't understand."

"I—I don't mean to say... Well, but..." Clearly terrified, she took a calming breath, closing her eyes briefly before squaring her shoulders and speaking again. "She...Earl Portsmouth went to seek her, and she made her demands."

"Do you agree with those demands?" Emmeline asked.

"I...I would never ask royalty to apologise to me, Your Highness."

"Are you of the opinion that I owe you an apology?"

"I..."

"Listen well, Lady Victoria," Alexander said, his voice a thin blade, quick to draw blood but never once losing its coolness. "My wife has told me about the lack of respect you have accorded to her father, and your designs on her brother. I am not certain of your opinion on the Lockharts, and neither dare I make any assumptions regarding how you view Emmeline and her father. Remember this, however – that she and I are joined not just in name but in heart. She is part of my family, and in so far as we think she has not erred in her ways, my mother, father, brothers and I will defend her at all costs. My wife and her legitimacy as princess will not be disrespected by any in this land."

Victoria dropped into a curtsy. "Yes, Your Highness."

"Understand that you will never exploit a hair on my brother's head as long as I live. And a word of advice for you," Emmeline said, her tone deceivingly light, "a lack of respect for others will never gain you any respect from others. To measure a person by the extent of their power and affluence is a shameful thing to do."

With that, the couple turned and walked away, satisfied with having put her in her place as they had intended to do. Their work was done. Meanwhile, Victoria rose shakily with a defiant sniff.

While the prince's cold warning had sufficiently concretised in her mind the exact magnitude of the authority and power the plain-looking girl commanded, she continued not to comprehend it. Surely she would not dare to speak condescendingly neither of nor to the princess and her family again, but she would continue her seething—how on earth had a girl like Emmeline Lockhart captured such devotion from a man such as Alexander St James?

***

"DAVID, I HAVE TOLD YOU COUNTLESS TIMES—"

"Georgeanne, you know I—"

"Duke Westchester!" Emmeline greeted merrily, unintentionally cutting David off. The duchess's stern glare, however, was enough to signal to her that she had chosen to appear at the wrong time.

Alarmed, she immediately turned to look at her husband with wide eyes, silently conveying a message. *Oh, dear, did I interrupt?—Was it rude of me?*

Alexander only smiled at her, snaking a reassuring arm around her waist, before he turned his gaze to the older couple. "Apologies, Duke Westchester, I certainly hope we are not interrupting an important discussion of any kind."

"Never, Your Royal Highnesses," David Arden replied with an obliging bow. Lady Georgeanne dropped the two a reluctant curtsy, and the younger two extended pleasantries in return.

"Is anything the matter, Princess Emmeline?" he then enquired, eyes as genuine as ever. "Is there anything I might be able to assist you with?"

"Not quite, Sir, I only wanted to introduce you to my husband," she answered. "I understand you have never met."

"No, Madam, indeed we have not." He offered Alexander another bow. "It is truly humbling to be in your presence, Your Royal Highness."

"A pleasure indeed," he replied with a slight smile. "I understand you are good friends with my father-in-law. Any friend of the Lockharts is a friend of mine."

Lady Georgeanne cocked an eyebrow at his courtesy. "That is quite interesting, Your Highness – I do recall you becoming rather upset when your father announced your betrothal. Clearly, your wife has done a splendid job taming you."

"This is my wife," David introduced hurriedly, "Georgeanne."

"Taming, Madam?" Alexander laughed heartily. "No, no, Emmeline has done nothing of the sort. As you understand, I was upset with my parents for depriving me of choice, but I did soon come to realise that my wife is not any more of a perpetrator in this than I am. It would be unfair to blame her at all for any of what transpired. Regardless of that, however...I did also finally see her for who she truly is – kind yet not without a fighting spirit, humble but not lacking pride – and I am grateful to have her by my side."

The princess flushed beside him. "He speaks too highly of me."

"Mm," Georgeanne hummed, as if to agree without actually agreeing.

"Hardly, beloved," he was quick to defend her. Then, turning to the older gentleman, "How do your daughters fare, Duke Westchester? My wife tells me you have five."

"Oh, yes, that I do," he said. "My eldest is due to be married – she has been exceptionally choosy with her suitors thus far, but my wife and I have one or two suitable candidates in mind."

"I understand one of them might happen to be my brother-in-law?" he asked, smiling pleasantly.

"Well, not—"

"Indeed," David interrupted his wife sharply, tone clipped. "We visited with Princess Emmeline and her family for lunch at Wellington House quite some time back. I would be most gratified if I might have Earl Portsmouth as my future son-in-law. I do fear, however, that my daughter has already offended the princess."

"I assure you that she has not, Duke Westchester," Emmeline said with a gentle smile dancing across her face. "I am not an individual so easily offended. There only exists, perhaps, a...clash in values. I worry that I am uncertain of how suitable Emmett is for her."

"Why, Your Highness, I could not agree with you more!" Georgeanne was quick to exclaim in reply, her viciousness carefully concealed, not a hint of it showing in her tone. "Perhaps another man might be more compatible with my Victoria. You know, she is far too used to the very highest of society."

David shot her an alarmed look, but the princess had already opened her mouth to defend her brother in the most courteous and, simultaneously, venomous way possible.

"Yes, perhaps it is so, Madam," she replied sweetly. "My brother might be too free-spirited for her – you know, he rather detests the overtly prim and proper."

"Well, Princess, our family—"

"Well, then, we must go, but all the best in securing your lovely daughter a good husband, Duchess Westchester," Alexander cut in, keen to bring his wife away before she gouged the duchess's eyeballs out with her bare hands. A fight was not within their designs for the evening; only well-masked warnings to the arrogant mother and daughter, and an agreement that no marital union should take place between Emmett Lockhart and Victoria Arden. Thus far, Emmeline and Georgeanne Arden had seemed to have reached some kind of consensus...that they should never be family because they bore equal amounts of dislike for one another. Neither future monarchs had anticipated the Arden pair to be so cooperative – and, in fact, enthusiastic.

Either way, he bowed slightly to the duke. "It was a pleasure meeting you, Sir."

His words were genuine. Georgeanne was awful through and through, but David was a truly nice man.

"I am honoured, Your Royal Highness." The nobleman turned to Emmeline and bowed deeply. "Thank you for making this introduction, Princess." He paused, and the silence was uncomfortable. "I do sincerely apologise if we find the union between my daughter and Earl Portsmouth to be eventually unsuccessful, Your Highness. Your brother is an exceptional man, and our Victoria would be blessed to be wed to him."

"Pray do not apologise," she answered warmly, her heart reaching out to this man who looked so sincerely saddened at the thought. "You can be blamed for no such thing. I have borne witness to your efforts...truly, thank you, on the behalf of my father." For first time in what felt like too long, she swept into a deep curtsy. "And you may address me simply as Emmeline, if it would so please you."

"Oh!" he exclaimed, "I dare not, Your Highness. I am but a duke, and you are to be queen."

Emmeline smiled. "Why, Duke Westchester, do you know me at all? I have never cared a jot for such formalities when it involves those close to my heart. You are one of my father's closest friends, and you are therefore one of mine."

He chuckled. "You are beyond fascinating, Emmeline." Then, turning to her husband, "You are a blessed man, Sir...but you were already aware of that."

With a courteous bow and curtsy, the crown prince and princess drew away from the older couple in relatively high spirits. They had completed their second task of the night. "I like him," she commented. "How regrettable that he will not become part of my family – do you not agree?"

"The wife truly is terrible, though – surely you do not wish to be related to her?" He smiled. "It matters not. I think I have sufficiently conveyed to her that you are very much a part of our family, and that we stand in solidarity."

"Yes, but David is wonderful. Truly, what a capital shame that we shall never know him as family."

"Well," Alexander made to offer her some sort of consolation, but his voice caught in his throat.

"...I wouldn't be so sure about that."

***

# Chapter Eleven

----------------------------------------

A /N Fun fact: it's Friday. I made time. Here's Eleven.

"WHAT?"

"I said—I wouldn't be too sure about that." He swallowed. "Look."

Emmeline turned, wondering what on earth could have frightened her husband thusly. Upon seeing it for herself, her eyes nearly popped out from their sockets.

Victoria Arden was all but hanging off poor Frederick, who looked most uncomfortable, his body postured away from hers, arm as far away from his side as he could hold it without being rude, and eyes scanning the crowd for anyone who could possibly help him escape the situation.

"Well, she was certainly speedy mending her shattered heart," Alexander remarked after an extended silence. "I would have thought she would be more anguished over losing your brother as a potential match...but, of course, considering that my brothers have since returned...well, I suppose I am not surprised."

Emmeline turned to meet his gaze. "Shall we rescue Frederick from her clutches? I feel rather sorry for him, look at the poor man's face."

He snickered. "You know, I am quite tempted to let him be. He looks so distressed."

"And you enjoy seeing him this way?"

"Why, of course," he answered. "Freddy always has his wits about him. In all honesty, it is quite amusing to watch him lose them."

"You are a cruel man," was all she said to him before walking towards her struggling brother-in-law. He chuckled to himself, but followed after her anyway.

"Frederick! Mother wishes to have a word with you," she said to the pale-faced prince. "I'm not sure what she wants, but she mentioned something about the lemon ices and a very upset lady."

"Mother? Truly? Well, excuse me, Lady Victoria," he said. "I must go."

Deftly pulling his arm out of her grasp, he slipped away into the crowd.

Victoria, looking very disconcerted, curtsied and also left with a small huff. Alexander offered her an amused nod as she went, barely succeeding in suppressing his laughter.

"Well," Emmeline said, turning back to him, "I imagine ridding ourselves of her shall be a challenge now, given that your brother is even greater a catch than mine."

"On the contrary, I think it shall not be," he answered, "if only because Freddy will most certainly not take interest in her, if his earlier misery was any indication of his will to take her as his wife."

"True enough," she conceded. "Very well. What else have we to do tonight?"

"Speak to your brother," he replied; then, grinning, "and dance to one more song."

She laughed. "Eager to dance with me, now are we?"

"You're a good conversationalist. I like spending time with you – in fact, as most people do."

She smiled. "Why, thank you. I'm flattered. If—" She was about to suggest dancing to the next song if it was slightly livelier than the current one playing, but froze suddenly as something – more specifically, a pair of striking green eyes just like hers – caught her gaze.

And then he was walking towards her, and although she had already intended to speak to him tonight to begin with, she felt the sudden urge to flee.

"Emmeline," her brother greeted, and she could hear her heart hammering in her ears. "May we have a word?"

"We may." She showed no intention to move.

"In private?"

She turned her eyes towards Alexander, apprehensive. In her plans, all three of them were supposed to be involved in this conversation, and she was unsure if she wanted to face her brother alone. She knew that he would never harm her physically, that he loved her too much to ever lay a hand on her, but he did not seem to know how to stop breaking her heart.

"Do as you must, beloved," he said encouragingly, warm blue eyes willing her to be brave. "Go. I will await you here and do my best not to miss you too dearly."

His joke lifted her spirits slightly. She swallowed, turning back to Emmett. "Very well. If you would follow me to my study, we might speak there."

She left the ballroom with him on her heels, and they made the journey to her private study in suffocating silence. She tried to calculate what to say to him, but she could only ever form half a sentence in her mind before it went blank again. The thought of how frosty their relationship had become made tears prickle in her eyes. It crushed her to feel so distant from the person she loved most on this earth, and it reminded her of the time he had so purposefully shut her out after she had admitted to her affections for Peter Jamison. He had been so resolute in his coldheartedness that she was unsure if she could win him over this time.

They arrived at their destination soon enough, and he shut the door behind them.

"What did you wish to speak about, Emmett?"

"Whom," he corrected her. "Victoria Arden."

"Of course," she responded bitterly.

His brow creased slightly. "What might you mean by that?"

"I assure you I meant no offence, only that that shrew seems to matter more to you than the relationship we used to have." Her tone was so flippant it surprised even herself.

"Emmeline, I would like you to understand my perspective." He sighed. "I am trying to do whatever I can for the family. I have caused so much disaster – so much pain to you. If Father thinks she is a strategic match for us, then I will pursue her, regardless of the repercussions that decision might have on me."

"You think that is selflessness, do you? You think causing me such heartache is selflessness? You think that disobeying direct advice offered to you from all three involved family members is selflessness?—If it truly is so, Emmett, you know nothing about selflessness."

"I will not claim to be a saint," he responded, "but I will do what I can for our family."

"Yes, do what you can – do anything but marrying that wench. If you truly wish to marry strategically and marry now, there are plenty of other women in the land for you to choose from. You cannot marry Victoria Arden!"

"Emmeline, I do not need my younger sister telling me who I can or cannot marry!"

"Oh! I see how it is now, Emmett Lockhart – you do not need my approval to marry, but I needed yours? I thought you loved me, and I thought you saw me equal to you – but perhaps, like every other man in society, you just see women as pawns in your game...even if they are your sister, and even if you claim you love them!" Tears of heartache and fury shone bright in her emerald eyes. "I have never blamed you for this, but—but you took the man I love away from me, Emmett, and I am not even allowed to help you choose a life that will make you happy?"

"And you say you do not blame me." He shook his head sadly. "I should have known that I never did have your forgiveness."

"You imbecile, you never had my forgiveness only because there was nothing to forgive! I have never faulted you for a thing. I owe you my life, Emmett – you gave me everything I had to lose. You gave me my happiness, my freedom...you bought me a cello. You taught me bravery. You taught me what it means to really love someone. And that is why I cannot let you marry someone out of guilt for whatever transpired with Peter – that is why this marriage will not take place as long as I am alive."

"Emmeline, I am a grown man with wishes that deserve to be respected, and my will is to—"

"Well, I'm sorry to say that your will does not matter, Emmett – at least it no longer does."

His brow crumpled immediately, eyes narrowing. "What do you mean?"

"I mean I have spoken to her and made my stand – and the stand of the entire royal family – clear. I have spoken with Georgeanne Arden and she agrees that the pair of you are incompatible. And I only just witnessed Victoria Arden hanging off Frederick St James's arm – in fact, I had to rescue him from her."

He pressed a thumb and forefinger to the bridge of his nose. "And what does Duke Westchester make of all this?"

"He said it is a shame. That he is sorry about it," she replied. "I doubt he will go to great lengths to salvage this match now, Emmett. The odds are stacked against it – nobody wishes for it to materialise with the exceptions, perhaps, of you and him."

"I see." He sighed.

"This is all over, Emmett," she said, with so much authority in her voice it almost rendered her unrecognisable to her brother, who was far too used to her loving and lively demeanour. "Given his desire for you to marry, Father is likely to seek you a different match soon. As we have done with the previous two ladies, we will evaluate her and proceed accordingly."

He ran a hand over his face.

"Very well, Emmeline." A pause. "I apologise if I put you through any pains."

She smiled tiredly. "Emmett, you know that I would endure anything for you."

But the princess had forgotten one key fact – that she was far from being the only Lockhart with a frustrating stubborn streak.

***

"DUKE WESTCHESTER!" EMMETT CALLED OUT TO DAVID ARDEN UPON catching sight of him later that evening.

David smiled, turning towards him with a beverage in hand. "Good evening, Earl Portsmouth."

"I heard about everything that transpired with my sister, Your Grace. I'm terribly sorry about it," he said. "I have tried to persuade her to allow the match, but she seems resolute."

"No matter." The older man smiled. "I am able to comprehend her intentions. She is only looking after your interests, Portsmouth – you must be grateful for her."

"I am, endlessly so," he replied, meaning what he said. "She is too good to me. She has always demanded that I have nothing but the best...I am fortunate to have her as a sister."

"As with most of the people in her life, it appears," he remarked. "I was speaking to the Prince and Princess earlier, and His Royal Highness seemed to share a similar experience with you."

"Is that so?"

"Why, yes. He was quite open in telling my wife all about their marriage and precisely how wonderful the princess." Duke Westchester chuckled. "Personally I did not require an in-depth explanation of their relationship, but I cannot blame him. Georgeanne seemed to wish to instigate some kind of response from them regarding their relationship, and he granted it to her."

"I see."

"Speaking of which, do kindly send Her Highness my apologies. My wife was less than courteous to her, especially."

"I will, Duke Westchester, although I will tell you this: my sister never holds a grudge. I'm certain she is not upset by it any longer."

"She is a lovely young lady."

"Yes, she truly is."

There was a brief pause. "Is there anything you need from me, Earl Portsmouth?"

"Actually, I would very much like to call on you at some point," Emmett said. "I regret that Victoria and I might not be married, but, in my capacity as an earl, I would still be greatly obliged if Portsmouth and Westchester might enjoy good relations."

"Why, you speak as if we do not already. Your father is a dear friend of mine. If there is anything you require in terms of your administration, you may write me without a moment's hesitation." His smile was kind, his eyes twinkling. "Although I will certainly not deny you a trip to my London estate. Will your father be joining us?"

***

I hope you liked the chapter - let me know if you did! Vote, comment, and share this story with your friends! :)

# Chapter Twelve

-------------------------------------------------------

A/N So sorry this is late!!! I hadn't even noticed Friday had gone by! Either way, I won't keep you any longer – enjoy the chapter! :)

"WELCOME, DUKE MAYFAIR. WELCOME, EARL PORTSMOUTH. HIS GRACE IS in the main drawing room. I have been told to show you the way."

The footman led the father and son through the main door, down a hallway and into a lavish room, where he bowed and drew away from them. The ceiling was higher than that of Wellington House's drawing room, and the rest of the room twice as bright. Everything seemed to be made of gold – a gold chandelier hung from the ceiling and gold sconces adorned the walls. The wallpaper was golden, and wooden parts of furniture were rendered a refined look with intricate golden inlay (detailing Bethany Rutherford would have loved). On the wall there was a portrait of a lady encased in a gold frame – she was far younger in the painting, but Emmett recognised her by her dark hair, dark eyes and alluring manner as the duchess Georgeanne. All the cloth cushion coverings were at least partly woven with golden thread. The whole room seemed to shine – it was certainly very expensive.

Contrasting starkly with it all was David Arden sitting in one armchair with a book. Dressed in a simple but smart grey suit, he was reading what Emmett recognised as a Jane Austen novel. Emmeline did also love reading those when she could. Their father, along with most men and a good many ladies, thought badly of books such as Austen's, but Emmett himself thought that they were good for women. They encouraged them to be brave and autonomous, in the very way he had always wanted his sister to be. Even if they did not, however, how much could a good love story hurt a woman's mind?

"Ah, William, Earl Portsmouth!" Duke Westchester greeted hurriedly, standing from his seat once he noticed their presence. "Welcome!"

"Call my son Emmett, David, I fail to see any need for formality between the two of you," Duke Mayfair replied smilingly.

"Well, how interesting – only last week at the ball your daughter asked that I call her by her given name, as well."

William laughed. "My daughter has never been one to stand on ceremony with any individual, with quite a lack of regard for status. Personally I reserve the use my first name for my closest friends and family, although I do not object to you addressing Emmeline by hers."

He smiled. "You Lockharts are wonderful people, William, truly."

"Well, the children must have inherited their amicability from Anne," he replied. "You know how she was like."

"Yes – without a shadow of a doubt, Lady Anne was the finest woman I have ever known."

"And the best person I have ever come upon."

Emmett stiffened beside him. Despite mostly having forgiven his father, his mother remained a sensitive topic he did not particularly enjoy discussing. Sensing his discomfort, David was quick to intervene.

"Would you fancy anything to eat, or drink?"

"Tea will suffice, thank you," William responded.

The finest tea in the house was sent for immediately, and Duke Westchester turned to smile at the youngest man of the three.

"So, Emmett, tell me about Portsmouth. If we are to concretise our relations, I must find out more about it."

"Of course," he replied eagerly, and began providing the duke with a thorough description of the earldom: its large population, its bustling trade, its amiable relations with other territories...most noblemen had, over the years, proved more than willing to form political alliances and trade ties with Portsmouth. It lay near the coast, and had much to offer in fish and salt. Its industrious and entrepreneurial people was another valuable asset. Literacy rates were high, and most were engaged in honest work, earning good money. Militarily, its strong ties to the dukedom of Mayfair meant that it was backed by William Lockhart's strong army, independent of the Crown, a very attractive factor to most other territories vulnerable to the whims and woes of the monarch.

And now, of course, that its earl's dear sister was to be future queen, Portsmouth was a more desirable ally than ever. The Lockhart twins were famously close, and many knew that falling into Portsmouth's good graces effectively equated to being on friendly terms with the ruling family. At the ball, nobleman of all kinds had been fighting for Emmett's attentions, scrambling to befriend the young man and have him remember their names.

"Well, I understand why you were so sought after during the Queen's party, then," David chuckled. "I noticed that you were rather...busy."

"Busy indeed," he agreed, grinning. "Well, Sir, do you think we might be in touch again?"

"Why, Earl Portsmouth, I think I could sign an alliance immediately. You know, for a lad your age, have quite the gift of the gab."

"Well, what a shame that I do not have the papers on hand!" he exclaimed, his elation evident. "I suppose I might just have to visit with you on another occasion."

"You are so very pleasant, my boy, you may visit with me on whatever occasion you would like. I never had any sons, you know, and I truly do enjoy conversing with you."

"Why, if you really do fancy him so greatly, David, you may keep the lad," William jested, and the three men burst out in roaring laughter.

Emmett delighted privately in Duke Westchester's invitation to call on him as and when he pleased to. This had played out exactly as he had wished it to.

***

FOLLOWING THEIR CONVERSATION OVER TEA, THE TRIO PROCEEDED TO Duke Westchester's shooting ground for an amicable competition in archery. The older men were proficient, admirably so for their ages, but Emmett was dazzling in his command of the bow and arrow. David was thrilled to invite him back for another afternoon on the shooting ground, and he was even more thrilled to accept.

Emmett and William returned home in the evening in time for supper. Over their meal, the older Lockhart remarked, "You have done well caring for Portsmouth on my behalf, son." He paused. "You know, I am proud of you."

The younger one smiled. "Thank you, Father."

"It would do Portsmouth good to form an alliance with Westchester. A very wise decision," he continued, looking down to cut a piece of beef on his plate.

"Thank you." This time, Emmett's smile was slightly strained.

"All for the right reasons, I hope." Eyebrows lifted, William placed him with a brief but meaningful glance before returning his gaze to his meal.

The smile disappeared altogether.

"I'm afraid I do not understand. What wrong reasons could there be?"

He swallowed his mouthful of meat and lifted his eyes to meet his child's. A barely visible smile rested lightly upon his lips as he responded in a manner no less cryptic than the way in which he had spoken the last time. "I don't know, son, you always have been the more innovative of us two."

Emmett's brow creased, but he said nothing, instead bringing his teacup to his lips and taking a long sip of his drink.

Despite his clear unwillingness to discuss it, his father did not change the subject. "Will you see your sister again while you are in London? I hear you resolved your dispute."

"Indeed we did, at the ball. Perhaps I will call on her this week."

"And who gave in to whom?"

"I to her, of course, as one would expect."

"Good. You know, your sister's probability of being right is alarmingly high."

There were words hidden behind the ones coming out of William's mouth, and he heard them all.

"Well—I do not mean to brag in any manner at all, but I did teach her much of what she knows. Therefore, one might suggest that perhaps my probability of being right is slightly greater than hers."

William chuckled. "I would not speak with such certainty, Emmett. Whatever most women might be like, Emmeline is far more rational than most men in the land. On this aspect alone her judgement already trumps yours."

"You quite offend me, Father. I am plenty rational."

"Fortunately or otherwise, I'm afraid that you are one who thinks with his heart."

"I—" The boy made an attempt at rebuttal once more, but was immediately interrupted. Rather unlike his own, his father's voice bore no argument – it was gentle and loving, something Emmett Lockhart was so unused to from anyone but his sister.

"To be guided by your emotions is not always a fault, my boy. To be blinded by it, however, could be your downfall. Let those who love you love you; if they should try to give you the best, do not turn them away. Your sister loves you, Emmett. Let her."

"I—"

"Goodnight, Emmett. It is late...I will retire now."

Instead of staying to bicker, William took one last spoonful of broth and stood. Passing his son by as he left the room, he clapped a hand over the the young earl's shoulder. It was firm and encouraging, and said things that he would never have had the courage to force out of his lips. I love you. We all do. Fight for yourself – you deserve it, son.

***

TWO DAYS LATER, EMMETT WAS, ONCE AGAIN, ON HIS MERRY WAY TO THE Ardens' London house. Duke Westchester was there to greet him at the door, and they exchanged bows, both gentlemen truly happy to see one another.

"How does your father fare?" David asked as he led the younger man towards the shooting ground.

"He is very well, Sir, thank you," was the reply, accompanied by a broad grin. "He sends his warmest regards."

"Do me a favour and return them. I do hope to see him soon."

"Of course." Emmett cleared his throat. "I hope your wife and daughters are well?"

"Yes," he answered. "Georgeanne is...as she always is, and so is Victoria. The younger few are all very good, also." He paused briefly, and for a moment all was quiet but the sounds of their boots crunching against the freshly-turned soil. "Speaking of them, I must apologise for my wife and my oldest's behaviour towards you and your family. I have been meaning to say this for a while now, but I was waiting for the right time."

He smiled courteously, shaking his head. "It is no matter. We love who we love, and sometimes a person's nature is not a matter of choice."

"Why – you are awfully wise for a lad your age, my boy. I have to say that I am impressed." David chuckled in the saddest way Emmett had ever heard another person laugh. "I'm afraid, though, that you are partly wrong. I will admit that it is the case for Georgeanne, but my Victoria – she has a brilliant mind and a heart of gold; truly, she does. But when you have a mother like she does..."

"Parents are very important in the development of a child," the earl supplied, his voice gentle as he spoke to this clearly heartbroken man. "I understand."

"Yes." Westchester sighed. "Of course, any rudeness she showed to William remains inexcusable. I only hope that you understand that she is not a wicked woman...that this is not her true character."

"I do understand, Sir. I assure you that my father, aunt and sister harbour no grudge towards her, nor towards you."

"Thank you," David replied, the two words simple but strikingly sincere.

Emmett said naught more, only offering him a warm smile. His mind, though, was hardly as silent as he let on – behind his bright green eyes and barely furrowed brow, the gears in his head were spinning, his mind racing with doubt. He wondered if Victoria Arden truly had a heart and mind as beautiful as her father claimed, if David simply thought too highly of a girl who meant the world to him.

Unlikely, he managed to persuade himself. He is a doting father. It should hardly come as a surprise to me that he would try to preserve his daughter's image...and even if he truly thinks thusly of her, no one in the world is more likely than him to overestimate the content of her character.

Yet his mind would not release him from rumination. It screamed with confusion – for what if David spoke the truth? What if Victoria Arden, whom he thought little more of than a common whore, was truly a human being with a spirit as worthy of protection as his own sister's?

It was unlikely – but on the minuscule chance that he did and she was, was it fair of him to bring her down with him in his quest to destroy his chance at happiness?

***

I hope you enjoyed this update! If you did, don't forget to vote and let me know what you think in the comments!

# Chapter Thirteen

- - - - - - - - - - - - - - - - - - - - - - - - - - - - - - - - - - - -

A /N The good news is, exams are over. The better news is, it's Friday and here's this week's update. Vote, comment, and share this story with your friends (it means a lot!)

"WELCOME BACK, LORD PORTSMOUTH," DAVID ARDEN GREETED MERRILY a few days later when Emmett had returned to the Arden estate on invitation from the duke. "My daughter is in the garden reading today. I hope that does not cause you any discomfort?"

"Certainly not, Duke Westchester – why, I would be happy to see her," he answered immediately, then cleared his throat hurriedly as he realised that he may have come off too eagerly. "What I mean to say is...I do not hold whatever failed arrangement we might have against her. I respect her as I do any good lady. This is her home, I am but a guest in it, and she may read wherever she pleases."

"A gracious young man indeed," David responded.

Emmett chuckled. "I am undeserving of your praise, Your Grace."

"Oh, enough with all these pleasantries. Simply call me Westchester like most of my friends do, or David if that pleases you better," the duke urged. "'Sir' sounds terribly stiff, do you not think so?"

"You are my elder, Duke Westchester, I could not possibly simply address you by your given name."

"Oh, come now, Portsmouth, I am hardly that old. Unless you insinuate otherwise?"

"...I would dare to do no such thing."

Both men burst out in roaring laughter. Despite his lack of regard for David's daughter, Emmett did quite like the man himself, and found the old duke an easy partner in conversation and an increasingly dear friend. There was no better way to explain it – Duke Westchester was simply a personable man in possession of great charisma, and Emmett liked him very much, as his father did. Having experienced David Arden for himself, Emmett was no longer surprised that the greying man with crow's feet and laugh lines was William's one dearest friend.

"Say, would you like to go for a ride in my wood today?" David offered. "It is quite an adventure, and if you enjoy a hunt, there is game to kill. You must be tired of the shooting grounds by now."

"I am never tired of archery, Sir, for your shooting grounds are wonderful – but I would never turn down a good hunt."

"Marvellous!" the duke sounded pleased. "Shall we proceed to the stables? I will fetch my gelding, and you can ride your fine horse. Speaking of that beautiful mare – what is her name?"

"Aurel," he replied. "I've had her since I was a young lad."

"You are still plenty young, my boy," Westchester said.

The earl laughed. "I suppose you are right."

They walked in silence for a while until David spoke again. "We will pass the orchard now, Portsmouth. Would you like to say hello to my daughter?—If not, it should not be difficult to slip past her...we will have to be careful with our footsteps, but that lass can get rather engrossed in a book. It is unlikely that she might look up if we do not call out to her."

"No, no, Sir, it would be a pleasure to see her. There is no need to hide from her on the grounds of her own home – that would, actually, be rather rude of me," Emmett was quick to respond. "I recall her telling us at dinner about how much she despises fictional literature. She must enjoy non-fiction, then. Does she find her mind engaged by that dry stuff?—I could never quite tolerate it for extended periods of time."

"Yes, that girl has always been a lover of the sciences. You seem like a sensible young man, so I will tell you this: I am quite proud of her for it, although she will never find a place in the field as a woman in our times."

"Perhaps one day – perhaps one day, things will change," Emmett offered with a slight smile. "Perhaps we will live to see it, even."

"I certainly hope so." David smiled back. "It would mean everything to my Victoria if she might enter the sciences professionally....till then, however, people tell my wife to get her away from her books and to the altar."

There was a sense of camaraderie between the two men now; both knew that they had a common desire – a common wish fuelled by the love for the women in their lives.

They walked on a little longer before the duke called out to his daughter as she came into view. "Victoria, darling!"

"Good day, Papa!" Her eyes seemed reluctant to leave the page, and she said this without looking up just yet. Then she tore her gaze away from her book, and, upon seeing the guest beside her grinning father, the light in her eyes faded substantially. "Your Lordship. What a pleasant surprise. I did not know that you had a guest, Papa...and did Earl Portsmouth not call on you only a few days ago?"

David raised his eyebrows slightly. "Now, darling, do not be impolite. He and I intend to sign an alliance...of course, the appropriate relations must be established before then. I think you may expect him to call on us quite often."

"I see," she said, not sounding very excited about this news. "Well, I very much hope you enjoy yourselves, Papa, but I should get back to my reading now."

She sat down and cracked her book open once more, and was about to begin completely ignoring them when Emmett suddenly remembered to force himself to speak to her before it was too late.

Regardless of what he might have said to his father and to Duke Westchester, this was the whole point of calling on David Arden so repeatedly, for the truth was that Portsmouth was more prosperous than it had ever been and had no shortage of allies. Now that a rare chance to interact directly with the elusive Lady Victoria had finally come, he had to seize it by the neck.

"What are you reading?" he enquired, the words nearly jumbling together as they flew in a flurry out of his mouth.

"Galileo," she answered simply.

"Are you familiar with much of his work?"

"I am, Your Lordship, I do take interest in his studies. That anyone might ever think the earth is flat amazes me ceaselessly."

"Some people still do," he remarked.

"Yes, and they are imbeciles," she stated blandly. "Any educated or well-travelled person would know that the earth is very round. It is rather impossible to fall off its edge."

His eyebrows raised in alarm at her bluntness. "Well, I suppose that is one evaluation of these individuals."

"You have another?" She cocked an eyebrow at him in a way that made him feel like an imbecile.

"I do, actually," he still found it in himself to say. "I think they merely have their own opinion, and they are as entitled to it as I am entitled to believing that the planet is round."

"That is no opinion, Your Lordship, that is an absolute falsehood! How could lies ever be valid?"

He paused. "I would not go so far as to call them lies, my lady...these people genuinely believe that the earth is round, and do not seek to spread falsity. Perhaps we might label them...alternative facts?"

Victoria's eyebrows crumpled immediately at his words. "I do apologise if this offends your sensibilities as one of the most polite and inoffensive gentlemen I know, good Sir, but I do believe that that may well be the stupidest thing I have ever heard."

Emmett laughed. "Fret not, my lady, I am not offended. If I may be candid with you, in fact, I think you are quite right. I am uncertain why I said what I did – it made me sound like quite the fool."

"Well, if you are asking for my analysis, Your Lordship, you said it because you do not wish to offend anyone," she said simply, as if he actually needed his rationale to be explained back to him. "You are an earl and a politician. Given that Portsmouth does have a good amount of rural area, it is doubtless that some of your people would subscribe to the belief that the earth is two-dimensional. Agreeing that they are imbeciles would not be a wise thing to do, even if it is unlikely that anyone will ever hear of this conversation."

"I think Lord Portsmouth is aware of his own decision-making calculi, darling," David said gently. "And if you would excuse us, I did promise him a good hunt in the wood. Enjoy your book, Victoria, and do not exert yourself too terribly."

She smiled demurely. "Reading is hardly exertion, Papa. I do hope you enjoy yourselves." She paused and turned her gaze to the young man standing beside her father, her eyes somehow not appearing as cold as they usually did although her tone remained quite condescending. "It was pleasant conversing with you, Earl Portsmouth."

"As it was talking with you," he said, and although he might never admit it to himself, the statement he had said for no reason more than courtesy was not so much of an alternative fact.

***

EMMETT KEPT CALLING ON DAVID ARDEN, AND DUKE WESTCHESTER appeared happy to receive him each time. More and more frequently Victoria would appear in the orchard when he called; and the two men would go to speak with her when they passed her on their way to the wood, the shooting grounds or one of the gardens to walk and discuss the specific terms of their agreement. She tolerated Emmett's constant presence, allowing him brief conversations each time he visited, and though she was a brash and direct as ever, he realised that she was a woman of great intelligence and vast knowledge. She valued truth above all and had a genuine interest in its pursuit, and she did not seem particularly evil – although she never did stop talking with a tone of voice that suggested her superiority over him. Her mother, on the other hand, was not blatantly offensive, but had a sinister air about her. Emmett could still remember his encounter with her – he did think that there was something off about her when they spoke in the Ardens' drawing room.

"I'll say, Emmett, my boy, you really are devoted to Portsmouth," Duke Westchester remarked when the earl once again arrived at his gates on horseback. "You must be the most frequent guest I have ever had in all my sixty years, and all for the sake of naught but an alliance with Westchester."

He laughed. "I certainly hope I do not bother you?"

"No, no, lad, never you," the older man was quick to reassure him, "you are a pleasure to have. I only fear our little town is not worth all your time."

"She is," he replied, hardly processing the words before he said them. Duke Westchester did not hear anything wrong with what he said, but he caught himself with a start and added, as if he had to justify what he had just said, "Westchester, uh, would be a highly advantageous ally for Portsmouth. You have an enviable level of economic productivity, one of the highest in all the land...my people would reap great benefit from your guidance."

"I am flattered." David smiled, and it was genuine.

"Pray do not be," the earl replied, recovering swiftly with a broad grin and falling back into his relaxed state of mind. "It is but the truth. Your land is one of the highest performing of all. It truly is admirable."

The two continued conversing in such a fashion, and Emmett managed to forget that he had ever said something that sounded so strange to him. *She is.* In any normal circumstance there would have been no question at all that he was referring to Westchester, the subject of their conversation.

Yet he had reason to believe that was not all he spoke of, and later that day when he had returned to Wellington House and sat with his father at the dinner table he found himself thinking of it again.

No, he told himself. No. I do not care for her in any such way. She is an intelligent girl, but every bit as repulsive as she has always been...and I still intend to marry her for the very same reasons.

God, I hardly know myself anymore.

He had always been fully lucid of all of his plans and intentions, but now he hardly knew why he was doing what he was. He did not know how he felt towards a woman he should still hate more than anyone in the world.

He needed something he knew.

The only person he knew better than he knew himself.

Then he remembered his father's advice to him a number of days ago, when Emmett had agreed to meet with his sister. Your sister loves you, Emmett. Let her.

He swallowed. "Father?"

"Yes, son?"

"I...I intend to call on Emmeline tomorrow."

William smiled. "I am happy to hear it."

***

# Chapter Fourteen

---

A/N Something sweet as an apology for the late update! I've been super busy this weekend...anyhow, here's Fourteen! Vote, comment, and share! :) -L

"GOOD DAY, YOUR LORDSHIP." THE GUARD DID NOT BOTHER ENQUIRING after his business or offering to give directions. All of Emmett's visits were for his sister, and he had long memorised the route to her study with the number of trips he had taken to it.

A curt nod was offered in response as Emmett rode on his horse past the palace gates and to the front courtyard. He dismounted and handed the reins to an approaching footman, then jogging up the steps in the direction of his sister's father study. He would surely find her there; it was where she spent all her time.

Much to his surprise, he found it empty.

He left the room, pausing in the hallway as he tried to decide where to proceed to next to seek her. Fortunately for him, a passing maid noticed him and his befuddled expression, and kindly stopped to help.

"Your Lordship. Her Royal Highness is in a conference with His Royal Highness Prince Alexander and a number of lords," she said.

"Do you know how long she will be?"

She paused to think. "Not long now, Sir, perhaps another ten or so minutes."

"I see. Have her meet me in the rose garden, will you?"

"I will convey the message to her lady-in-waiting, Your Lordship."

"Thank you." He nodded in appreciation, and she curtsied hurriedly before continuing down the corridor. He began on his way to the rose garden, strolling in the opposite direction. He allowed himself to go slowly, admiring the grandeur of the palace. Floorboards were crafted of the finest wood and polished to perfection, gleaming in the light of the chandeliers overhead. There was a mural painted on the ceiling overhead, telling awe-inspiring legends of kings and queens past. The walls were painted a light cream colour, adorned with gold sconces holding unlit candles. To his left were a line of doors, all exactly the same size, shape, and colour, made of wood similar to the kind used for the flooring, only unpolished and half a shade lighter. There were no labels on any of the doors, and Emmett wondered in awe how on earth the servants and royals of the palace differentiated between all the rooms. Perhaps he would ask his sister later.

His sister...He chuckled. Given her character, he was sure that she did not think much of living in the palace. Surely she would have gawked when she first arrived to visit the Queen for tea so many months ago, for it truly was stunning, but living here...she was never a woman who needed luxury in her life. It amused him somewhat how the woman chosen to marry the prince and take on his opulent lifestyle was one of the few women in the realm who would not appreciate it.

Victoria Arden, on the other hand... he allowed himself a sardonic chuckle. She would love a life like this.

He never expected, just a few minutes after bearing such a thought, that he would encounter the chocolate-haired lady herself.

Emmett Lockhart was only about three dozen paces away from the rose garden when he came face to face with her – it all happened so suddenly and so shockingly he was nearly knocked off his feet. He was looking forward to seeing his sister under amicable circumstances, for he did love her deeply regardless of his own hidden intentions and the foolishness from which they stemmed.

And then he saw her.

He froze at first. He watched her eyes widen in terror and her hands tighten over one another. Surely it was a trick of the light. What business might she have in the palace, in the home of a princess who hated her so?

He blinked, and still there she stood, quivering like a mouse.

"Lady Victoria," he finally greeted her. "... What brings you here?"

"Oh – only some...business," she replied lamely.

"With whom, might I ask? There is a meeting in procession – is Duke Westchester here? Did you come with him?" He seemed not to notice her discomfort.

"Papa is not here," she choked out. "I came on my own...to see—to meet with one of the barons—with one of the baronesses at the meeting. My mother sent me."

"Ah, I see," he answered. Then, puzzlement struck him with some suddenness and cocking his head, he enquired, "I was told that only lords were involved in the meeting. Which baroness do you speak of?"

"I—" Something caught in her throat, but then she seemed to remember something, and automatically her chin lifted, her hands went to her sides, and she straightened to rise to her full height. "I'm afraid I have to seek her now, Earl Portsmouth, and I cannot stay to make this frivolous small talk with you. Good day to you, Sir."

And she glided past him like the haughty lady he knew her to be.

***

"GOOD MORNING, EMMETT," SHE GREETED, EYEBROWS ARCHED, "WHAT A pleasant surprise."

She had received his message to meet him in the rose garden, and found him waiting among the yellow roses.

He rose to greet his sister. "Hello, Emmeline."

She sighed. "Surely this is not about Victoria Arden again? I already—"

"No," he hurriedly clarified, "it is certainly not. I do not wish to think of her a minute longer than I already have. It has only been too long since we have met on amicable circumstances, and I miss my sister."

"I have missed you, too," she admitted. Then she paused, and he sensed that the entire tone of the conversation was about to change.

This would not be the merry encounter he had intended for it to be.

"Why, Emmett, do you keep appearing as a stranger? I know you are reckless, but you keep forcing these terrible things unto yourself...unto all of us. Why are you so insistent on making me cry, time and time again?"

"Emmeline, I do not mean to hurt you, I only—"

He expected to have some kind of rational explanation, a long, sincere emotional appeal as to how his actions were driven by his love for her. He expected to know exactly what his motives were, exactly how all his actions were driven by his love for his family...

But he did not.

One tear rolled down her cheek, pain written all over his face, and he felt a pang in his heart. He had caused this...all of this.

"Emmeline, my dearest, I am sorry. I really am."

"Are you sorry? Are you? You have done this so many times now, Emmy. It hurts me...it hurts my heart. A lot. I...I do not know how to help you. I do not know how to save you from yourself." Her voice quietened within the short span of a few words, and she turned away from him, almost as if to hide the grief blazing in her eyes.

"Linnie, I..."

She faced him again, brows crumpled, eyes shining, an image of defeat and exhaustion. "Teach me, Emmett – you have taught me so much. You have taught me to help myself, to live my life for my own sake and not for anyone else's benefit...Now teach me how to help you."

When he said nothing, a sob escaped her throat. "Why are you behaving this way? Why are you so...self-destructive?"

"I...I deserve Victoria Arden."

"Emmett, you hate her."

"And I hate myself." Those four words simply fell out of his mouth – he had not meant to say them. But they were the truth. For the first time in so long...he was telling his sister the truth.

It felt like liberation. It felt like happiness for the first time in months. He had shut her entirely out of his life. He had deprived her of access to his innermost thoughts, when she had once upon a time been the one to know them all.

Let those who love you love you. He could have sworn then that he heard his father's voice by his ear. Your sister loves you, Emmett. Let her.

"Emmett..." Her voice was gentle then, and he knew telling her had not been a mistake. It could never be.

He sighed. "I am sorry, Emmeline, truly I am. For everything. For what happened with Peter and for everything else I have done to hurt you. I promise I never wanted to be the cause of your grief...and I know you have forgiven me, for you never fail to remind me of it, but for the life of me I cannot forgive myself."

She came to stand before him with a bittersweet smile. She took his hands in hers, and the small gesture send a wave of warmth washing over him instantly. She always did have an uncanny ability to soothe him, her calming effect a balm for his wounds.

"Let me help you."

Momentarily he remembered just how much he loved her – he had let his guilt and rage over his past folly consume him, driving him onto a mission to ruin himself, guided so strongly by his own grieving heart that he had forgotten to feel the love he shared with her – his sister.

She had meant everything to him, and she still did.

"Thank you."

She laughed. For the first time in a long while, she laughed in front of him and meant it – her eyes still glimmered and her cheeks were rosy, but her face was captured with an expression of pure happiness.

"Oh, Emmy, you know there should be no pleasantries between us."

She leapt into his embrace. Surrounded by blossoming yellow blooms the Lockhart twins were finally reunited – in the truest way possible, not merely in the physical sense like they had already been before, but in heart and mind.

***

EMMETT WAS SOMEWHAT SURPRISED, PLEASANTLY SO, TO SEE HIS ROYAL Highness Prince Alexander standing side by side with his sister as they greeted him at the palace gates a number of days after the siblings' reconciliation, engaged in what looked like merry conversation. She was laughing and he was smiling affectionately at her, and if one knew no better, they might assume that the pair was in love.

He jumped off his horse and handed her to a footman. When Emmeline caught sight of him, she tore herself away from her talk her husband to throw her arms around him in a hug. Chuckling, he offered her a pat on the back in reciprocation before drawing away.

"What an honour," he jested in greeting, "to be met with by both royals before I've taken more than two paces onto castle grounds."

"I could not wait to see you," Emmeline explained animatedly, "and Alexander did not wish for me to stand outside alone."

"Well, then, thank you for taking such care of my sister, Your Highness. It is reassuring to know that she is loved here," Emmett said, grinning broadly at his brother-in-law once the slightly shocked expression had gone from his countenance. He had not expected the pair to be affectionate with one another at all – the last he remembered, Emmeline had mentioned her husband keeping a respectful distance from her. When had things changed? Had he truly been too wrapped up in his own self-destruction to notice?

Had everyone truly moved on but him?

"Please, Sir, it is only Alexander to you," was the gracious response with a sincere nod in return. "And pray do not thank me. Caring for Emmeline is naught less than my duty."

Then she cleared her throat, reminding them both that she was standing right with them. "All right, gentlemen – it is wonderful to hear how loved I am, and I hate to interrupt your conversation, but shall we go indoors? I am getting quite chilly."

Alexander chuckled. "Of course. Let us talk in the drawing room."

And so they did, the princess walking arm-in-arm with her husband and her brother standing on her other side. As the three talked and laughed as they walked, she truly did feel like a princess, and for a moment felt incredibly lucky to have settled into such a blissful life. Finally everything had reached a stable equilibrium – her relationship with Alexander, while not a dramatic love story, was one of a close partnership, and her issues with Emmett had been resolved. Her father wrote her often and she was always glad to pen a cheerful reply. With each day that went by, she saw more and more of her mother in her own face. Her life was more complete than it had been in a long while – or, in fact, than it had ever been all her life, and she was grateful for it.

***

# Chapter Fifteen

----------------------------------------------------------------

A /N Warning: drama ahead. Brace yourself!

THE THREE TALKED FOR A GOOD HOUR BEFORE IT CAME TIME FOR THE twins to proceed to meet with David Arden at the Arden house. They would be travelling there on horseback, and Emmeline in particular was thrilled to finally go riding with her brother again. It had been far too long since they had last gone galloping into the woods by Lockhart Manor together with the wind in their faces and laughter streaming from their lips, and she was grinning as she stood to announce that she was going to change into a riding habit.

Penelope was in her bedroom when she arrived – there was a pair of black leather gloves already laid out, and she was holding a pair of boots in her hand, eyes flitting between the two as she puzzled over whether they were the best options possible to find in Emmeline's selection of accessories.

"Ah, my lady!" she greeted merrily, relief flooding onto her face when she saw the princess standing at the door with an amused smile on her slightly tinted lips. "What colour would you like to wear?—Are black gloves and boots all right?"

The princess laughed. "I think I would fancy powder blue today. The gloves are fine, Penny, and those boots are lovely. Thank you."

And so the lady in waiting retrieved the necessary articles of clothing – a tailored shirt, a formal jacket and a long skirt, all in the delicate shade of azure which had been requested, coupled with a matching top hat which had a veil attached at the brim and an fragile-looking gold necklace to complete the outfit. The necklace was a chain of small golden flowers, and it had been Lady Anne Lockhart's before it belonged to the princess. She helped Emmeline change out of her dress and into the habit, assisting her with her gloves and shoes as well. Then she braided her black hair, pinning little blue flowers in it after she was done. Then the hat went onto the princess's head, the veil not concealing her smile.

"Thank you, Penny," she exclaimed, "I look wonderful!"

"My pleasure, my lady," the younger girl replied with a bright smile to match Emmeline's. "I have instructed one of the stable boys to lead Allegro and Aurel to the gate. We will meet Lord Portsmouth there."

"Excellent, Penelope. I can always depend on you to arrange things so splendidly." She was still smiling softly as she stood. "Shall we be on our way now? I should not like to be late."

The duo went on their way to the gates, where Emmeline ran to greet her lovely black stallion. He seemed happy to see her, snorting as he buried his nose in her shoulder. She laughed, running her hands up and down his sleek neck affectionately. He was a stallion, but never aggressive towards her. She had, after all, been the one to save him from castration when he was but a wee colt, throwing herself over him when she herself had only been but a child and begging her father not to harm him. "Maybe I should castrate you, too, Father, for the danger that you might one day lay a hand on me!" she had shouted, hot tears streaming down her cheeks. She was but a child, and did not know what castration truly was, but she knew that it would involve taking a knife to the poor horse, and that it only happened to males because of their temperament. The statement made his father's heart soften and his lips twitch in the direction of a grin (for, despite his better sensibilities as a grown nobleman, it was after all quite amusing to hear a wee lass threatening to castrate her own father), and he found himself left with no choice but to give in to her. Since then Allegro had been her charge – for William Lockhart had decreed that she would bear responsibility for any wrong he might ever do. After all, his possible aggression would have been a direct result of her pleas.

The stable boy, who was holding the reins, switched the halter for a bridle in preparation for the princess. Allegro was already saddled, and the prospect of being ridden by his beloved mistress again after so long made him stamp his hooves against the cobblestone in anticipation.

Emmett, on the other hand, had already mounted his lovely white mare Aurel, reins in hand, and grinned broadly at his sister when she hoisted herself up upon her grand stallion completely of her own strength although the stable boy made to help her up. Since she would be making an appearance as a princess on horseback, she would be riding sidesaddle, although she usually did enjoy very much riding astride when she was alone with her brother in the wood by Lockhart Manor. Yet the preposterous notion that her modesty would be compromised should she ride like her brother did prevented her from doing so whenever she was in public, and however much she detested this baseless restriction upon her freedoms atop a horse, she could do little about it. For the sake of her name and her family's honour, she would have to ride sidesaddle in public.

She took ahold of the reins and nodded at her brother, signalling that she was ready to go on their way to David Arden's fine estate. Eight palace guards were waiting nearby – they were to follow the siblings, also on horseback, to guard the princess's safety. Three would ride behind them, three would flank either side, and two in front.

Thus the party set off, the twins in high spirits and their horses equally pleased to be out and about together again. Commoners rushed out of their cottages when they passed, lining up along the street to gaze curiously upon them. Mothers seized their daughters eagerly by the arm as the Lockharts rode by, whispering in their ears: "That is Her Royal Highness Princess Emmeline, my love, and you one day must be just like her." For all had heard of how very brave and true she was, of her wit and the purity of her heart. She was not as pretty as most princesses had been, and in most cases this might have been a disadvantage for a woman in her position. Yet this only made her seem like less of a stranger to the masses, and it made all the mothers in the land even more eager to produce daughters as virtuous as she.

"Why, Linnie, you seem quite popular," Emmett remarked with a chuckle.

"But of course," she answered playfully, "I am the sister of the great Earl Portsmouth, after all."

He laughed, louder this time, and she joined him, bursting into her own peal of ladylike giggles.

"Thank you, by the way," she said once they had both recovered.

"Whatever for, dearest?"

"For telling me about this," she clarified, "about your...designs with Duke Westchester and Lady Victoria. And then for inviting me along on this visit. It means a lot that you might be so honest with me."

"And who else might I be so honest with? I love no one more than I love you, Emmeline, truly – no one," he replied. "I promise never to deceive you again. I really am sorry, you know, more than anything."

Emmett had confessed everything to her in the rose garden – of his tactic of accessing Victoria Arden through her father; of the conversations he had

had with the girl; of how he had begun to despise her less; of how confused he was. She had smiled at him in her reassuring way and given him the answers he needed.

"Well, if you are asking for my opinion on the matter, Emmett, no one person is all good or all bad, but individuals are usually either mostly pleasant or mostly unpleasant. In my view Victoria is mostly unpleasant, and she may he an intellectual, but she is certainly an intellectual snob. That she might refer the uneducated as imbeciles is rather indicative of her attitude towards them, and I do not think you should like to marry a woman who thinks lowly of the underprivileged."

Currently they rode to see David Arden together. Emmeline had ordered the palace solicitor to assist in writing up the agreement, and soon it would be signed and Emmett would not have to see Lady Victoria for much longer. Then she would find him a wife, a good one, one who did not think of those who did not read Galileo as imbeciles and one who could match him in spirit and love.

It was a while longer before they arrived at the Arden manor. When they finally did, Duke Westchester was there to greet them. "Your Highness! Portsmouth! Welcome."

"Good day, Duke Westchester," Emmeline answered smilingly as she dismounted (without the help of the footman who had held his hand out to assist her). "It would suffice to call me Emmeline, you know."

"No, no, Princess, it would not." Despite his formality as he said this, he grinned amicably at her. "You are royalty, Your Highness, and I am your subject. I will address you as I should."

She laughed resignedly. "Very well. If that would be what pleases you most."

There was a brief silence as Emmett also got off his horse, and the footman took Allegro and Aurel away.

"Come, now, a good ride through the wood awaits us after some tea," Westchester said, and they began to walk toward the house. "Did your brother tell you of the thrilling hunt we had some days ago?"

"Yes, he did. It must have been great fun."

"Oh, it certainly was so," he answered. "Do you ever hunt, Your Highness?"

"I have accompanied my brother on a few," she said, "although I myself am not quite comfortable with taking lives thusly."

"Why, but your middle name is Artemis, Your Highness," the duke pointed out. "She is the goddess of the hunt, no?"

She laughed. "Perhaps she is, but I am no hunter. I am quite fond of animals, actually, and I rather prefer keeping them alive."

"Oh, Emmeline is so good with animals, Duke Westchester. My dogs are more hers than they are mine, and she was the only person who could tame her lovely stallion Allegro," Emmett interjected.

"My, what a gift. A well-kept secret as well. I never knew that about you, Princess," he remarked as they arrived at the main entrance, and footmen pushed the large doors open for the three. They talked idly as they walked toward the main drawing room, until Emmett was suddenly interrupted by a shrill shout.

"How many times must I tell you, Victoria, you are the finest lady in the land and will behave as such! I do not care how you feel towards Prince Frederick – whether you want to marry him or not, you will make him love you, and you will be princess!"

A desperate cry rang out. "Mama I—"

"You are my oldest daughter and your father's most prized child, Victoria, you would do well to remember that! You deserve nothing but the very best, and with that snake Emmeline Lockhart already wed to Alexander St James, Prince Frederick is the best to be had!"

"I am not like Emmeline Lockhart, Mama, I have no desire to be married to a royal for the mere sake of it! You said this yourself—she married Prince Alexander for the fortune and the power, but I am hardly as shallow! I would sooner be a spinster for ever than marry a man I do not love!"

"You are not like her, Victoria, you are far superior, but since that wench has already robbed you of your place as queen the least you could do is seize a position second in line!"

There was a brief pause before the girl was heard again.

"But I lo—"

"Enough! Defy these orders again and I will have all your books burned!"

Then there was ear-shattering silence, and both Lockhart siblings froze in shock. Victoria Arden was being coerced to seduce the prince? An image of her draping off Freddy's arm came to Emmeline's mind. Had that all been Georgeanne Arden's doing? And Victoria's poor attitude to the princess – had that too been fuelled by her devilish mother? There seemed to be some grave misunderstanding caused by things the duchess had said.

Despite the fact that she still strongly disliked the snobbish lass, Emmeline felt deeply sorry for Victoria Arden. She herself did not have a mother to speak of, but to be "blessed" with one so vicious...

"I apologise for that," David said after an extended awkward silence. "For having to hear Georgeanne having one of her fits...and for what she said about you, Your Highness. It is...quite unforgivable."

"Well, um, well," she said, still in shock, "I...I do suppose she is entitled to her opinion of me. Do not apologise for her own views, Duke Westchester. Her...Her mind is quite independent of yours."

Emmeline plastered a smile back onto her face, but in the privacy of her mind wondered about what Victoria had been about to say.

She had certainly been about to confess having feelings for someone else.

But who?

***

Dun, dun, dun...tell me what you think is going on! There'll be hints here and there in the following chapters. Comment at any point on who you think the mystery man is!

# Chapter Sixteen

A /N What's up? This week's update, that's what. Vote, share, comment, the usual! :)

THE ALLIANCE HAD BEEN SIGNED.

Duke Westchester seemed happy to agree to all terms after his wife had unintentionally insulted the princess to her face, and Emmett was not about to complain about his readiness to do so. Yet he could not help but wonder...had David been right? Was Victoria's dislikability truly a product not of her own nature, but of her appalling mother? After overhearing how horrible her mother had been towards her, he had developed substantial sympathy toward her. Perhaps she was not as bad as both him and his sister had believed.

Either way, it no longer mattered to him. He would not be marrying her, nor would he continue to associate with her. His sister had been quite right – she was not pure evil, but no one ever really was. He mostly disliked her and that was ample reason to steer clear of her. He would not speak with her ever again...and her relationship with her mother was her own business.

Meanwhile, Emmeline, too, was troubled by the newfound information about Victoria Arden, and, one fine evening, brought it up at the table as she dined with her husband's family.

"...and so I am no longer sure how to think of her," she explained. "I have always viewed her poorly, but now that I know of her circumstances, it is difficult to dislike her with the certainty I had before."

"Why, my dear, forget her," Sarah suggested. "Harbour no ill feelings toward her, and think no more of her."

"What about Frederick?" the princess asked, and the man in question looked rather green. "Georgeanne Arden has her heart set on making Victoria second in line. She will not let her leave us in peace."

"We shall ignore them," was the matter-of-fact reply from the matriarch. "The girl herself has no interest in Freddy, only her vicious mother. This is reason enough not to respond to any request for a union they might pursue."

"I do wonder, however, who might own Victoria Arden's heart," Emmeline hummed, in deep thought. "She was no doubt about to confess her love to another. Who?"

"I do not imagine he might be—"

"I do not understand your need for idle gossip such as this," Prince Javier snapped, interrupting his mother and shocking everyone at the table. "This is why I so dislike being home, Mother, and it is only worse with this girl in the house. I will never understand why women behave like such giggling idiots."

Alexander's expression turned stony immediately. "Javier, I must insist that you treat our mother and my wife with the respect they deserve—"

The younger prince narrowed his eyes. "What, brother, has marriage changed you so quickly? Have you been so thoroughly enraptured by your lovely wife that you might jump to her defence so quickly? Only weeks ago you would have been happy to agree with me!"

Alexander's hackles raised instantly, and Emmeline placed a hand on his arm to soothe him. Before he could shout back, however, his father cut in.

"Enough!" King Andrew thundered. "Javier, we sent you away hoping you would learn to be less rebellious. In this aspect your brother has grown immensely, but you seem to remain the same obstinate child! Perhaps we must find you a bride also!"

"Father, I refuse to be chained to a woman!" Javier shouted.

King Andrew's eyes narrowed. Refusing to engage with his son in a full-fledged argument, he lowered his voice to his normal volume. Yet somehow he sounded even more threatening when he spoke quietly. "Well, son, neither did Alexander, and now he is perfectly content with his wife."

"He is to be King. I shall never be! May I not act as I please?"

"No, you may not, Javier, you are a royal and you will act accordingly! I would not have raised the issue of finding you a bride before you started throwing your childish tantrum, but you must stop your philandering ways!"

"Married or not, I most certainly will not." He stood abruptly. "I have lost my appetite. Good night, everyone."

And with that he stalked back to his quarters, leaving the two women to stare after him, shocked and dismayed.

***

"ARE YOU ALL RIGHT?" ALEXANDER ASKED GINGERLY, STEPPING INTO HER quarters and shutting the door gingerly behind him. She had retreated here not long after Javier left, claiming to feel slightly unwell, and he suspected that there was naught wrong with her body. Her discomfort was in her heart.

"Yes, Alexander, quite fine," she replied, looking up at him as he entered.

He smiled softly at her. "Come, now, you need not pretend in front of me."

"It is only that your brother detests me," she said with a sigh. "Javier."

"He does not detest you, Emmeline, he treats everyone that way," he replied. "Truly. We all had a difficult childhood, and we all responded to it differently."

"Difficult?" she prompted, hoping that he would tell her about it.

"I'm sure it is nothing compared to losing a doting mother at a young age, but..." He sighed. "Being a prince is harder than it looks. Our father never really loved us and our mother was always busy with important affairs. She is very intelligent, you know, and very involved in politics and the like.

"None of us ever felt loved. I was put under immense pressure to prepare to be King, and the others always had to be on their best behaviour. We never had a chance to run and play and just be children, and it took its toll on all of us. Being the eldest, I was coerced to conform the most, with higher expectations than the rest. I came to resent the system upon which our society is built, and my parents as well for their negligence.

"Frederick responded well. He never quite lost his positivity but learned to be the perfect son to our parents. To this day he has not spoken a word against them – he is the golden boy of us four, and my mother loves him the best out of us all. Father favours him as well, although he really is not affectionate to anyone but Mother.

"Lionel, our youngest brother, became excessively meek. He hardly speaks, especially in this household, and, in essence, has no opinion on anything."

"Oh, I met him once," Emmeline agreed. "I was with my brother in Portsmouth. Emmett certainly did all the talking, now that I think of it, but back then I merely assumed your brother was simply a good listener."

Alexander chuckled, shaking his head slightly. "That is one way to see it, I suppose."

"And what of Javier?"

His face fell a little, then, and she could see that his brother's newfound ill behaviour hurt him greatly – more than he would show her. Nevertheless is cleared his throat and squared his shoulders, trying to appear as unruffled as ever.

"He shut us all out. Perhaps it is unsurprising that he did not talk to me, but he would not even speak to Freddy, who is always so pleasant, nor Lionel, who would never hurt him with his words. He fell into vice – when he turned ten and six he began to drink, when he turned ten and eight he began to...he began to lie with many women. It is all very scandalous...most of this the people do not know. For how would they think of their ruling family then?" He laughed bitterly. "My family is dysfunctional. One would hardly consider us fit to lead an entire empire."

She placed a comforting hand on his arm. "Oh, Alex."

He turned to her with a resigned smile. "Feel no sympathy for me. Perhaps I have sinned terribly in lives past. This must...This must be some kind of retribution. There must be no sadness over it."

"Oh, pray do not say that."

"If my theory is correct, however, then I must also have done some tremendous good...for why ever else would God have sent you to me?"

His wife's ears turned pink. "You flatter me."

This earned her a chuckle, genuine and filled with all his usual humour that she had grown to appreciate so much. "Goodness, we must look like a couple."

"How appalling," she jested.

"Indeed. The thought of being romantically involved with you is absolutely repulsive, beloved." The glimmer had returned to his eye.

She giggled. "I shall be sick if I am not rid of you this instant."

"As shall I." He stood, grinning now. "In truth I shall be sick should I ever be rid of you, dearest, but I should go. It is late and me staying any longer would be improper."

"We are married, Alexander, you may stay however late you like. No one will talk, even if we do nothing else."

"I am well aware of that. Besides, there are few who possess the audacity to insult me with their wagging tongues," he replied. "But I leave out of respect for you. You must not be comfortable in the company of a man so late in the evening."

"Well, that is quite moving," she said, rising also. "The truth is that I think little of such dogmatic societal norms, but I thank you for other reasons. I should like to rest soon."

"Then I hope you sleep well." He pressed a kiss on her forehead. "Goodnight, Emmeline."

"Likewise. I will see you tomorrow?"

He nodded with a slight smile. "At breakfast, or before."

She smiled back. "Lovely."

With that he left the room, ducking out of her door in a fashion quite reminiscent of a man sneaking out of his lover's quarters late at night. But she was no lover to him – their relationship was not so illicit far more scandalous, for she was the girl chosen to be married to the Crown Prince and she had not laid with him once. With this thought haunting her mind, she stared at the closed door he had left behind. She was a princess and one day she would be Queen. She was certainly expected to bear him children, but how on earth could she ever bring herself to do so?

After all, they were not lovers of any kind. They were friends and partners at best. Her heart still belonged to Captain Peter Jamison. Her heart still belonged to her lover – and he was far, far away.

She wished Peter had been the one to duck discreetly out of her room.

She wished she could see his face again. She wished she could feel his hands holding hers, she wished she could feel his chest rise and fall under her cheek as she simply sat with him, serene and complete, truly happy.

She swallowed these desires, closing her eyes tightly to stamp the image of his hazel eyes out of her mind. She knew this was irrational. She knew this was wishful thinking. She had long accepted her life entrapped in the palace walls...she had long known this to be her reality. She had fallen into an easy routine, grown used to Alexander, grown somewhat affectionate toward him even. She often found herself quite content with the lot she had drawn, and it truly was for the best that she might feel this way. There was, after all, no alternative reality available to her.

Yet for all her intelligence and level-headedness, she sometimes still found herself thinking of another time and another place in which she might have married her dream come true.

In these moments she would close her eyes and erase his image from her mind. It would return in due time, but she was a royal now. She had responsibilities, and one of them was not to think of another man while wed to the Crown Prince. Of course it did not help that Alexander was trying so hard to make her happy, to be the husband she wanted and nearly had, the Peter Jamison she missed so dearly...

Perhaps in another life. Perhaps in another era and another land she might find true happiness.

It simply would not be this one.

*** 

# Chapter Seventeen

---

Remember when these used to get posted on Wednesdays? Well, here's a little extra surprise to help pull us through Hump Day! :) x Leanne

"I WILL BE OUT OF THE PALACE TODAY," EMMELINE IN-FORMED HER husband at breakfast a week later. "Father has scheduled for Emmett to meet another potential wife. I hear she is rather agreeable, although her father is baron to a less wealthy area. Perhaps this might spare us some snobbery."

"Perhaps," he agreed. "I wish you all the best of luck."

"Thank you." She smiled. "I will return as soon as I can."

"You can tell me about it then," he said.

She nodded. Had finding a man a wife always been this difficult, or was her brother somehow jinxed?

"Emmeline, dearest, you should invite your brother over for luncheon or dinner sometime. We would all love to have a good meal with him, since the two of you share such a wonderful relationship. In fact, I would not mind having him over today, after your business with his marital prospects."

Javier grumbled at this assumption. No one paid him any mind.

"I will extend your invitation to him, Sarah," she replied politely. "Thank you. He will be flattered."

"And he will accept, hopefully," the Queen said eagerly. "Does he prefer chicken or beef? Or any other meat, for that matter?"

Emmeline laughed. "Emmett is fond of all foods. He has never been picky."

Sarah beamed at her. "Excellent, then, we shall have some of each kind!"

"That will prove a very tempting offer to him," she laughed.

The rest of the meal was uneventful. An hour after the royals finished breaking their fast Emmeline Lockhart was out of the palace gates in a carriage, on her way to Wellington House. She was glad to have been granted freedom to enter and leave the palace as she wished. Before she married Alexander she often worried she would be literally caged. Now she saw that it was all metaphorical, though not much better. For a princess must behave as a princess should, and Princess Emmeline you should not do this, that, or the other...it certainly helped to have a husband as free-minded as hers, who viewed her as a person rather than a possession, but she was still very much at the mercy of the wagging tongues of the ton and public humiliation.

Her father stood at the gates of his estate, ready to greet her when she arrived. She offered him a slight curtsy and a brief embrace, which he returned affectionately.

"Where is Emmett?" she then asked, drawing away from him.

"In the drawing room," he replied tiredly, "with the guests."

"Oh, goodness, I do apologise for being late." Her eyebrows were up to her hairline as she realised that she had left her father and brother to deal with the intricacies of hosting guests in her lateness. Yet she must not have arrived much later than she was due to, for she had been brisk about her preparations and quite efficient, and with any luck, the lack of a woman of power in the house would not have frightened the guests quite yet.

William smiled at her, as lovingly as ever, but it was clearly strained. "You are not a minute late, dearest, they are early."

She frowned. "Is something wrong, Father? You seem absolutely exhausted."

"Nothing," he said with a chuckle. "Come, now, and see for yourself."

She did as she was bidden, and followed her father into the drawing room. There she found herself in the presence of the most ostentatious gown in the world, doubtlessly purchased to impress. It was a tacky shade of orange and full of frills and crepe, paired with gold jewellery which might not have been genuine. The girl wearing the dress had a remarkable amount of makeup on, and her entire head of flaming red hair had been curled into alarmingly large hoops framing her slightly rounded face.

Emmeline looked tiny next to her, in a simple pastel blue gown with her hair simply styled, and as white as a sheet.

But perhaps her paleness did not come about as a result of the juxtaposition.

"Why, what an honour. Your Royal Highness, I am humbled indeed to meet you." The baron greeted upon seeing her frozen at the door, rising to bow to her.

"An honour, Your Highness," the girl was quick to imitate her father, differing only in that she curtsied instead an enthusiastic glimmer in her eye although the words came out as quiet as a mouse.

"Oh...good day to you, as well," she said. Emmett squirmed uncomfortably and shot her a wide-eyed look at screamed please save me from this madness. She cracked a smile at him, forcing herself not to laugh at the panic upon his face.

"Yes, hello, Princess," a plump woman trilled from the side of the room, and as Emmeline turned to look at her she knew immediately who had done up this poor girl for the meeting. It must have been her mother, dressed just as tastelessly in a deep purple. She curtsied earnestly, wobbling.

"H-hello." Emmeline smiled politely. "Shall we...shall we sit and talk?"

***

EMMETT LOCKHART EXHALED WITH RELIEF WHEN THE DOORS CLOSED behind their over-the-top guests. "Please never write them back, Father."

William laughed. "I shall not. Imagine dealing with them for the rest of your life."

"Dear Lord, no." The earl laughed also.

Emmeline smiled as she watched them jest among themselves. Truly, though, she was deeply sympathetic toward the girl. She might have been elegant in another life – she had a pleasant voice and pretty eyes, but her parents seemed far too eager to impress, and had forced this upon her also.

Then, she asked, "Emmett, will you return with me to the palace? For luncheon? Sarah invited you."

"If you would like me to."

"I think I would," she replied. "Perhaps we could assess one of Alexander's brothers together – Prince Javier. He seems to detest me, although Alex promises that he detests everyone."

"He does," Emmett assured her. "I met him once. He detests me also."

"What consolation," she replied dryly.

"Linnie, you cannot win everyone's favour. There will always be those who attempt to sink your ship."

"Are you challenging me?" she said, her eyes narrowing ever so slightly.

"Am I?" He grinned roguishly at her.

She thrust her chin up at him. "I accept. Watch – he will like me. One day."

Emmett hitched an eyebrow. "If you are indeed able to win his favour, Emmeline, I shall be most impressed."

"Enough to make a wager, brother?" She grinned.

He paused to consider it. Then, "However highly I think of you, my dear, you are on the wrong side of this gamble. Very well. Should you truly earn his liking, I will give to you five hundred pounds to spend as you please."

She smirked, pleased with herself and overflowing with confidence. The money was purely tokenistic, for she would never squander such a sum. In fact, she was unlikely to even accept it in the event that she won it; but victory would taste sweet on her tongue.

"Let us go now to meet him, then."

***

"THANK YOU FOR ATTENDING, PORTSMOUTH," KING AN-
DREW SAID AT THE table later that day, as the young Earl sat beside
his sister before the royal family. "My wife Sarah really did want to meet
you properly."

"Your invitation flatters me, Your Majesties," he replied, as charming as
ever. "And, of course, this wonderful meal. I am hardly worthy of such
splendour. Truly, thank you." Just as Sarah had promised, the finest meats
of all varieties lay spread across the dining table in reception of the young
man, the oldest wines retrieved from the cellar to enjoy. Emmeline had
been shocked to see such an extravagant welcome prepared upon their
arrival (for she had sent a man ahead not too long ago to notify the royals
that Emmett would be coming with her to the palace), Sarah had looked
terribly pleased with herself, Alexander had smiled brightly at her and
offered an affectionate kiss on the knuckles, and Javier looked as angry as
ever.

"Both twins share the same courtesy, I see." He smiled, pleased.

"We shared a governess," he explained. "Miss Paltrow was...terrifically
stern."

"Well, she seems to have done you both plenty of good," the monarch
replied. "Perhaps we might employ her when Alexander and Emmeline
bear children? Which we certainly all look forward to very much."

"Father, please, none of this talk," the eldest prince urged in a low tone
when he sensed his wife stiffen slightly beside him. "Not now."

The King raised his eyebrows at him, asking with some incredulity in his
tone, "Well, son, what else might we talk about?"

"What about you, Earl Portsmouth?" Sarah jumped in hurriedly as she
noticed the Lockhart twins start to fidget in their discomfort. "Emmeline

seems to be heavily involved in arranging your marital affairs recently. How is that for you?"

"We met one possible candidate today." He offered a tight-lipped smile. "A lovely girl, but she was...not the one for me."

"Absolutely disastrous," his sister chimed in, "rather pleasant, as Emmett says, but her parents were flamboyant to a fault."

"Did you not say that she is from a less affluent family?" Alexander asked, eyebrows lifting in surprise and curiosity as he turned to look at her.

"I did, and she is," she answered with a tired smile. "My theory is that that made them all the more eager to please."

"Oh, dear," Frederick said. "Surely, however, better than Victoria Arden."

"Shall we discuss something else?" Prince Lionel suddenly suggested, surprising everyone by speaking since he rarely did anything of the sort. "To be most honest, I...I do not think Lady Victoria good table conversation."

"Actually," Queen Sarah disagreed, "I am indeed curious to know – what is your opinion of her, Lord Portsmouth?"

"I have no opinion of her, Your Majesty," Emmett replied. "I am afraid that I do not know her all that well."

Javier looked straight at him then, brows furrowed. "And yet you wanted to marry her? I hear you even attempted to pursue her through her father, no?"

"And how do you know all this, brother?" Alexander asked sharply in return, eyes narrowed at the hostile younger prince.

"Victoria Arden is all you talk about at the dinner table – of course I would know everything about all of your dramatics involving her."

Alexander huffed, admitting silently that his brother was not quite wrong (although he would never have done this out loud). They did indeed converse about matters regarding Lady Victoria Arden and her family at the table rather often, seeing as she was the only thing that had united the family in a very long time. Nonetheless she was beginning to divide them again now, and perhaps it was time to return to their customary polite silences and stiff, brief discussions about the kingdom's affairs. He hated reverting to this after feeling like a family for once in so long, but he supposed that it might have been better than Javier throwing violent fits every time they started to talk.

"I think Lionel is right – we should not discuss Victoria Arden any longer. It does us no good."

"Finally someone sees sense," Javier muttered.

Emmeline smiled apologetically at her brother, sorry that he had to witness the ugly cracks in this family's bonds. He shook his head slightly at her, telling her it was no issue at all...he had only seen one disagreement, but she had to live with these people.

She turned back to her food, though she poked and prodded at it more than she ate it since her appetite was mostly gone. As she shuffled her food around her plate, she could not help but think of what Javier said, what he knew, and the reason he had provided as to why he knew all that he did.

"Victoria Arden is all you talk about at the dinner table – of course I would know everything about all of your dramatics involving her." That had been his argument, and it had seemed sound to everyone else...everyone but her.

She sighed slightly. But I never brought the issue of Emmett pursuing Lady Victoria through her father up at the table.

***

A/N Hi everyone :D Thanks for reading! Leave me a vote if you liked this update and, as usual, please let me know what you thought about this chapter in the comments. Don't forget to tell me all about your theories on the ongoing mystery - I'd love to hear what you guys think! :) See you all again on Friday! x Leanne

(Confession: I'm slightly worried that I've made it way too obvious by now, haha...)

# Chapter Eighteen - PART ONE

-------------------------------------------------------

A/N Hooray for updates – two in a week! :) Chapter Eighteen is something of an origin story and will have to stretch over two chapters. I hope you guys enjoy this peek into the deepest darkest chambers of Prince Javier's heart! As usual, vote, share, and let me know what you think about this chapter (all feedback, positive and constructive, are welcome), and see you next week! :D

SHE SUCKED IN A BREATH BEFORE RAISING HER FIST TO KNOCK ON THE door that would lead to Javier St James's study. There was a long pause before she received any kind of response. It had been a week since she had had Emmett visit for luncheon and a week since she had spoken to the younger prince, and though she was tempted to be annoyed with his standoffishness she found herself somewhat grateful that he might answer at all.

She had come to win her bet – but more than that, she had come to touch the heart of a broken soul. He was not a bad person, only injured...she knew it. No brother of Alexander's could be rotten from the inside out.

His father, on the other hand...

She shook this thought out of her head. Her focus must be on Javier now. Perhaps she would be able to redirect him to a better path – one on which he had a future of stability and happiness. She knew that – even though he was prince – he had not drawn a particularly desirable fortune in the birth lottery; but neither had she, and she had found a way to be content...

"Who is it?" the beast within grunted, his disinterest clear.

"It is me, Emmeline," she called back. "I'd like to speak with you, please."

"Well, I have no desire to speak with you." His words might have been hurtful to someone more egotistical, but she took no offence, instead breezing onward with her enquiry as if he had not said anything of the sort.

"May I come in?"

No reply. She waited for ten counts before asking again, doing her best to keep her voice light and pleasant.

Finally seeing her persistence, the voice on the other side of the door finally relented, sounding quite tired. "...Only if you promise to leave quickly."

"All right." She pushed the door open to see him, surprisingly, hunched over a book. "What are you reading, Prince Javier?" she asked, in an attempt to be amicable; but she should have known that amicability was not appreciated in the least in this room.

He snapped the book shut and tossed it aside. "It's none of your business, and please just call me Javier. I despise the title. Now what do you want?"

"To talk," she replied. "I only have one simple question, really. Why do you dislike me so much?"

He scoffed. "I have no interest in discussing this with you."

"Well, I have all the interest in the world—"

"How many times do I have to tell this to people?—I don't care." He sounded irritated, a clear sign to Emmeline that he did indeed care. She had known it all along. He was human...he was only hurt.

"Are you angry that I married your brother?" She was gentler now.

He, however, did not soften. "No. I don't care who Alexander marries."

"You do," she urged him. "I know you do."

"I. Do. Not," he replied, his eyes cold and hard as he stared right through hers. "You know nothing about me, sister, but here is what I know about you. You are an overprivileged woman who grew up safe and loved. Your brother showed you happiness and freedom. You enjoy a wonderful relationship with your father and brother today...I, on the other hand, I have never known any of this. Safety, love, happiness, liberty – these are all luxuries to the likes of me. I have known hardships you have never even dreamed of. You have no right to stand here and lecture me—"

"You think you know so much about me, do you not? You think you know all about my life, about the things I have or have not been through?" Suddenly she raised her voice, her eyes narrowing. She had not come here to fight...but he had made her snap. He had, knowing nothing about her, made assumptions about her childhood – he had called her safe and loved! What did he know?—Who, truly, was he to much such a false claim?—

"You think you know me! Do you know my mother died when I was six? Do you know I saw her body? I saw her eyes, empty, and I cannot forget them! My own mother, dead in front of me! And then my father – my father did not so much as look at me for the next six years of my life! Instead he hired this horrible woman who tried to twist me into a person I was not as if she could ever replace having a father. My brother had to take me away from him when I was of age simply because I was so miserable! I know you did not have a perfect childhood, Javier, but that you should have the audacity to claim that I did—!

"I will tell you that I was happy for the next five years. I was finally free, living with my doting brother in Portsmouth – still robbed of a childhood but, at least, free. I learned to live and to love and to laugh, to be happy despite everything, and then your family came along. I was in love with a man, I really was, but I was forced to marry your brother...I loved him, I still do, deeply and more than anything in the world – Captain Peter Jamison of the Royal Navy, my brother's dearest friend. Do not think yourself the only victim of your father's cruelty; he threatened Peter's post. He said that if Peter ever saw me again, he would never see the ocean. And you claim that I know freedom more than you do?"

The silence hung thick in the air between them, and the only sound in the room was her breathing, heavy from the exertion of being so angry with someone. Yet finally he found it in himself to speak.

"I..." Javier closed his eyes and exhaled, sounding defeated and, perhaps, truly sorry. "I apologise. I was rude."

"No, Javier, you were not simply rude, you were absolutely insufferable," she replied harshly, standing from her seat in front of his desk. "I wanted to help you. I wanted to help you feel happy. You would not let me. Perhaps some people will be miserable forever... Perhaps Emmett was right after all. I can't make everyone like me, even if I only want the best for them."

His brows creased slightly as he looked up at her. "Thank you very much, but I am happy."

She laughed. "Believe me...you are not. I have known a sufficient number of miserable people to know it." Then she turned. "Good day to you."

She crossed the room in wide steps, ready to leave and leave this man alone forever. Then she heard him call her name, "Emmeline, wait!", the words sounding funny coming from his lips. He had never addressed her directly before.

"What do you want, now?" she asked, not turning to face him. She had no doubt that not all his hostility was his own fault, but she knew that she had to recognise that some men were broken beyond healing.

"If you would sit down...perhaps I might tell you my story, too. Then we may decide together how insufferable I am – or, at least, how unforgivable."

***

PRINCE JAVIER ST JAMES HAD NO MEMORY OF BEING WITH HIS PARENTS from his early childhood – or, for that matter, all throughout his life. Who he did remember, however, were Greta, a seasoned maid who lived with them in the palace, his three brothers, and his tutor Mr Fitzgerald Claymore.

Greta was like a mother to him – she was like a mother to all four brothers, really. She had been put in charge of caring for the princes, as one of the Queen's most trusted servant, and had been there for every scraped knee and childish drawing while Her Majesty was preoccupied with more important things. Despite her kindness towards him, the sight of the slightly aged woman still brought a sharp pang to Javier's heart, for she was a reminder of everything she did not have. She was the closest thing he had ever had to a mother, and she was not his mother...he did not have a mother, not a proper one, anyway.

As a young child, he was frequently puzzled. He experienced great sadness over his parents' absence in his life, and yet his older brothers seemed mostly unaffected. (Lionel never confused him – the poor boy practically lived his life quaking in his boots. He was most definitely permanently scarred by his parents' poor performance as parents.) He would often look them over at the dinner table when they supped as a family, the only time they were all together except when they prayed in the chapel, observing them and their strange lack of grief.

Alexander, the eldest, was always bickering with their father, opposing everything he said and every rule in the castle. "Do you not think this system dogmatic?" "Do you not think this method flawed?" "Father, has it never occurred to you that this belief of yours is downright idiotic?"—He seemed to enjoy the quarrels, never showing a single sign of sadness, always ready to fight. It almost seemed as if it made him happy that his father was such a poor one, and he did not talk to his mother much except when she hurried to Andrew's defence.

Frederick – the second child – was a golden boy, a perfect child, a mediator. "Come now, Alex, let us fight no longer. The soup is cold." "Forgive him, Father, he meant you no offence." "The rose garden is beautiful, Mother, I passed it today and the flowers look lovely." He was Alexander's spitting image, only that he did not look quite so angry – he always wore a smile and seemed so pleased with everything and everyone regardless of how little their parents actually showed concern for them. He seemed at peace with the fact that their parents did not love them – he lived fully in spite of this fact, something Javier was never able to understand.

"Say, Li," Javier had once asked his younger brother, his one true confidante, "do you ever get sad about Father and Mother?—how they never talk to us?"

"All the time," Lionel had replied quietly.

"Me, too." He'd paused to think. Then he had asked, "Do you think Alex and Freddy care at all about how cold Father and Mother are?"

"I...I don't know," had been the response. "What do you think?"

"They seem so...unaffected. Alexander is always angry and Frederick is always happy. I have never seen them sad – not once."

Lionel had stayed quiet then, either of no opinion or too afraid to speak it, and the conversation came to an end, leaving Javier none the wiser.

# Chapter Eighteen - PART TWO

------------------------------------------------------------

Every minute of every hour, I miss you, I miss you, I miss you more.

THE LAST PERSON JAVIER KNEW AND KNEW WELL WAS HIS TUTOR, MR Claymore. Mr Claymore was not a handsome man, but the prince thought him to be the cleverest man in the world. He was a man of science, and he knew everything about everything – he knew about plants, about animals, about the lands and the seas and everything else Javier had never seen. He also knew about who Javier really was, a detail no one else had ever put in the effort to see. Beneath the façade of a brooding, sulky prince was a small boy craving the love of his father and mother, the guidance of his older brothers, and the warmth of a functional family. There was also a brilliant man waiting to blossom.

"You could be a man of science, Your Highness," Claymore had once said to him, a fire in his eyes. "I have tutored you as well as your brothers, and though they are all very intelligent, you are exceptional, even among their ranks. I have never been a big believer of fate and destiny and all the likes, but you were born to know the world – as I was. I...I simply know it."

Momentarily, Javier's heart leapt at the prospect of having a destiny like Fitzgerald Claymore's. As far as he was concerned, anyway, his tutor was an outright genius, a prodigy, a hero. These words made his eyes shine even brighter than Claymore's, if that was even possible, as he listened intently.

"I think you should consider going into further study – Oxford, perhaps, or Cambridge. The professors there might teach you better than I can...a fter all, I did learn all I have taught you from them."

University!

This could mean so much for him... It could mean an entirely different life! In science, doing the things he loved, instead of in politics like his father wanted...the thought of sitting in court, the prospect of wasting his life away in tedium and misery, sickened him now that Mr Claymore had said that he was meant for greater things. That he was exceptional...surely this would be enough to persuade his father?

Father—! Father will never agree to this, it suddenly occurred to him. Immediately he deflated, his face falling, his hopes and dreams plummeting from his chest to the bottom of his stomach. Father is intent on all four of us becoming a part of running this country...he wants us all to dedicate our lives to it! He shall never agree to let me study! For the briefest of moments he had been filled with the strongest desire he had ever felt, and it had been followed by the strongest regret he had ever experienced. Oh, how much he would have given...

He voiced this concern to his tutor, who only smiled kindly and replied, "It never hurts to try, Your Highness. If you should so desire to...we may speak to your father His Majesty about a visit to both universities. I would be happy to take you – we could speak to the professors, for I am closely acquainted with some, and perhaps even listen to some of the classes...we could return to the castle within the fortnight."

"He would never listen, Mr Claymore, even if you should attempt to persuade him," Javier said, brows furrowed in desperation and despair. "Father wishes all four of us to join politics."

A sly glimmer appeared in the older man's eye. "What about Her Majesty?"

"What about my mother?" Javier asked, confused.

"And I thought you were clever, lad." Claymore laughed. "Have you not noticed your father's pattern of behaviour, Your Highness?"

"He has always been very stubborn, Sir."

"Except when...?"

The prince's brow remained firmly furrowed. "I...I don't understand."

Claymore sighed. "Except when your mother persuades him otherwise, Your Highness. Your mother is the one person in the world who can convince him of anything at all."

His eyes lit up at this realisation. "Yes!...and surely Mother will let me pursue this path – she always says she wants us to be happy. Science will make me happy!"

The tutor smiled. "Excellent, Your Highness. Do notify your parents of my desire to speak to them at some point soon, and let me know when they would like to discuss your future."

Future. For once, Javier St James felt like he had a future and not merely a fate.

***

A WEEK LATER, THEIR MAJESTIES KING ANDREW AND QUEEN SARAH, HIS Highness Prince Javier, and Mr Fitzgerald Claymore all sat in one of the castle's many drawing rooms.

"You would like to discuss my son, Mr Claymore? Something about his future?" the King was stern as he asked this question, even to a man no younger than he was himself.

"Yes, Your Majesty. I have observed in His Highness outstanding talent in the sciences, and I would like to suggest a two week trip to the great universities of our land, Oxford and Cambridge—"

"We appreciate the sentiment, Sir, but there is no need. My son will join me in court when he is grown – any further education in the sciences you might be trying to propose will be unnecessary." The King offered a slight smile, as if to soothe the harshness of his words, but it was cold and insincere.

The tutor frowned slightly, angling himself toward the Queen instead in a change of tactic. "Prince Javier is a truly exceptional student, Your Majesties. I have never seen one quite like him. It would be a great waste not to allow him to reach his full potential."

"Mother, please," the boy jumped in at once, eager to support his teacher, "please let me go with Mr Claymore. Science makes me happy – it is the only thing that has ever made me happy."

"You will find equal levels of fulfilment in court, son, no need to fret," Andrew cut in sharply before his wife could speak a word in response to his son. "It was what my grandfather did, and my father, and now it is what I am doing; I assure you there is plenty of joy in running an empire."

"But Father, court is so boring! What joy could there be in that?" Javier cried.

Andrew turned livid instantly. "I dare you to say that one more time, boy!"

Mr Claymore turned to Sarah, turning desperate. "My Queen, please."

"I..." She looked between her husband and her son, clearly torn. "Andrew ..."

In response to this, the King only huffed. "My answer is final. No. Javier, you will remain in the castle."

"That isn't what I want, Father!"

"It doesn't matter what you want!"

And that, as it turned out, was the young prince's breaking point.

He stood from his chair, jaw tightened, eyes hard. "All my life, neither of you have ever showed me a hint of affection! I have never, in my entire life, had a father to teach me to shoot or ride or hunt, nor a mother to pick me up when I fell. If you will not give me love at all, perhaps I might forgive you. But since you will not let me be happy in this home, why will you not let me be happy elsewhere? Do you simply want me to be miserable for the rest of my life? Was robbing me of my childhood not enough?"

"Javier, please calm down," Sarah begged earnestly. "Sit, son, please."

"No! Don't you tell me to calm down – don't you call me your son! You have been an absolute failure as a mother!"

Something flashed in her eyes. It was not anger, that was in her husband's steely glare...heartbreak, perhaps, a realisation that she had, truly, been a terrible mother to her four most beloved children.

"Your Highness, this is not the way," Mr Claymore urged. "Have a seat."

Only then, and very begrudgingly, did Javier return to his original position on his chair.

"Prince Javier...please apologise to your mother."

"No," the boy refused, adamant. "If anyone is owed an apology, it would be me."

In a lower voice meant to soothe, the tutor tried again. "Please, Your Highness, remember what we discussed."

Yet this only backfired miserably – and even Fitzgerald Claymore, the man with infinite wisdom, could not have foreseen it.

"Yes, pray, Mr Claymore, enlighten us – what did you discuss?" the King demanded. "Conniving with my rebellious son, are you, Sir?"

"Of course not, Your Majesty." He looked up at the King, not a trace of guilt to be seen in his face. "I am not a man to connive, as you say it, and your son is, most definitely, not a rebel."

"Ah, you know him very well then? More so than I might know my own child?"

He sighed. "That is not what I meant to imply, Your Majesty, I pray you do not misunderstand."

"No, Mr Claymore, my father seems to have understood perfectly," Javier disagreed, defiance burning in his eyes. "You do indeed know me far better than he ever will, if only because you would take time to speak to me!"

"Your Highness, stop."

"And such control you have over him!" Andrew exclaimed with sarcasm dripping from his words. "Do tell, what poisonous seeds have you planted in his mind?—This ridiculous idea of my son becoming a man of science must have been yours, yes?"

"Andrew—" Sarah laid a hand upon his arm then, and Fitzgerald felt himself begin to breathe easier. This was what he had intended to happen.

"No, Sarah. This vicious man has been feeding Javier horrible thoughts. He should thank me for letting him off so easily – I could have him hanged for treason!" Turning to the tutor, then, he said, "You are dismissed, Mr Claymore. We will not expect you here again."

"But what about my lessons, Father, you cannot—"

He narrowed his eyes at the horrified boy. "Believe me, Javier, I can, and I will. All this science has done you no good. You will no longer require classes."

Then, calling to one of his servants, "You, there! Call a guard to escort our good Mr Claymore out of palace grounds...and have all of Prince Javier's books burned. Every last page – he needs no more distraction from them."

As a palace guard arrived in the room to haul the one man who truly knew him out of the room, Javier felt every last drop of blood in his body turn cold.

He would never let his father have his way. He would be hanged for treason before he would comply.

***

A/N Poor kid :( As per usual, vote, share, and comment - let me know what you think of Javier now! x L

# Chapter Nineteen

---

A /N Happy Friday everyone! And an early Eid Saeed to any Muslim readers I may have!

Okay, down to business. The first chapter of this paragraph would have been the saucy part, but I think I have successfully un-saucified it. Of course this still implies that a man and a woman spent the night together, but I think I've made it safe for young readers. If you happen to be one of those young readers, I've done my best to make it child-friendly. I think this is as non-sexual as it gets.

As for my other readers, do let me know if you think it's okay to put it back on #SafeLove (or if you don't, haha).

Here we go!

"WHEN ARE YOU GOING TO TAKE ME AS YOUR WIFE?" SHE ASKED HIM AS she laid in his arms, bathed in the rich colours of dawn that seeped through the gaps in his heavy drapes.

"I never promised you marriage," he said, drawing back from her, incredulous.

"What?" she shrieked. "But you must—! I assumed—It is doubtless – eventually I will be with child. And who will answer for it then?"

"I...I will consider it."

Despite his near concession, she remained slightly hysterical. "Why do you hesitate? Are you ashamed of me? If you are, I will remind you that I am the eldest daughter of a wealthy duke – there would be no shame in marrying me."

"I know," he replied simply, untangling his arms from her and swinging his legs off the bed as he rose. "I am not ashamed of you, not at all."

"Then I do not understand the complication!"

"The complication is that I am not meant for marriage," he said as he clothed himself. "Hurry up and dress. You must leave soon."

"You know, I detest our arrangement," she complained, even as she obeyed. "With all this sneaking around, I feel like some sort of – oh, I feel like some sort of criminal!"

"Then why do you stay?" he asked, oddly calm and not even looking at her, his gaze affixed on the buttons on his shirt as he did them one by one.

"Because I love you," she said plainly. When she received no reciprocation of sentiment she reiterated it, a little louder this time, a little more plaintively. "I love you!"

He was silent for a full ten counts. Then, in a low voice, he said, "Put on your dress and go, Victoria, I mean it."

"Am I... Am I not enough for you?" she asked, her voice quivering. He did not turn to look at her – he knew she was on the verge of tears, and he had no wish, then and there, to console her.

"No," he said. "You are far too much."

Then he made his way towards the door. "I have other business to attend to now – an important meeting. Leave as soon as you can...there will be trouble if a member of my wait staff finds you here."

"What trouble could there be but—"

He slipped out the door before she could even finish her sentence.

***

EMMETT LOCKHART STRODE QUICKLY OUT OF HIS QUARTERS, BOUND FOR the main door. He had to attend a gathering with some other prominent noblemen in the palace this morning. He had not broken his fast yet, but Emmeline had promised him a delicious meal together once he was finished with his business.

As he passed the drawing room, his father called out to him. "Emmett, son, I bear good news! I am in contact with a marquess with a fine daughter!"

"Excellent, Father, thank you," he called back, although he harboured different thoughts in his mind. Marriage, he mused. Perhaps I am not meant for it – perhaps it is not meant for me. I have always known that I do not want it as other men do, but now that every attempt I have ever made at it have been such failures...

The stable boy had Aurel ready and waiting at the door. Not wishing to ride huddled in a carriage on a day as fine as this, he mounted the horse instead and started her on a steady canter toward his sister's home. He regretted slightly the fact that she would not be the first person he had an engagement with – rather, he would have to sit through a tiresome meeting with who would probably be some stuffy old men before he could see Emmeline's face and hear her refreshing laughter.

He handed Aurel to a footman when he arrived. She stamped her feet, and an unknowing passer-by might assume her unwilling to leave her master; but Emmett was familiar with his mare, and was aware that she was only excited, for every time she came to the palace she would be taken to Allegro while she waited for him to finish with whatever he had come here to do, and she adored the black stallion just as strongly as Emmeline adored her older brother.

He proceeded on his way to one of the palace's secondary drawing rooms, where he was greeted by a room full of idly chatting nobles. A crier announced his arrival, and those in the room greeted him either with subtle nods or formal bows, depending on how their status compared to his. He offered a courteous bow to all in the room, smiling as charmingly as he always did. He had a good many friends in the room – that was, after all, how he brought Portsmouth to unprecedented prosperity.

An arduous two hours later, the Lockhart twins met in Emmeline's private study for breakfast. There was a trolley equipped with two trays of food sitting by the desk when Emmett knocked gently and entered, and his sister, not in her grand, throne-like chair behind the desk for once, sat in a plush chair to the side of the room, examining a document in a simple champagne pink dress, her eyebrows creased ever so slightly in her concentration. She did not notice him come in.

"Good morning," he greeted, shutting the door gently behind him.

"Ah, there you are," she replied, smiling as she put her papers down on the small table in front of her. "How was your meeting? I hear that its outcomes have large impacts on Portsmouth's future – hopefully it went well for us, then?"

"It was just fine, dearest, Portsmouth will not be having any additional tariffs imposed on its trade. I was able to convince the other lords that it would be beneficial on the kingdom as a whole and more agreeable with the royal family, although – judging by their faces, anyway – I think they would very much have liked to drive merchants away from our little port for their own profit," he answered.

"How impressive, Emmett," she cooed, equal parts teasing and genuinely congratulatory. Then, far more jokingly than sincerely, "Father will be terribly pleased, no doubt – you have saved us all once again!"

He chuckled, shaking his head slightly at his sister's theatrics. "Thank you, Emmeline, but enough about my morning. What is that you were just looking at? You seemed rather engrossed by it."

"Oh, nothing that significant – only a slight amendment to the law that is being proposed in court," she said. "Alexander is having me look it over."

"An amendment?" he asked. "Why are you looking it over?"

"Because I am an intellectual no lesser than he," she replied, sounding slightly offended. "Brother, you of all people—"

"No – you misunderstand," he cut in hurriedly. "My question is, why can he not do his own work?"

She sighed. "Shall you always think ill of him?"

"As long as it involves you, Linnie, yes, I will think the very worst of him until I am proven to be wrong. I should not like to assume you are not being exploited or hurt – for what if you are?"

"He is not doing anything of the sort, you silly goose. In fact, it really is quite the opposite." She handed him the document to see for himself. As he scanned over it, she continued her explanation: "Alexander wrote this, all of it – a proposal for women to be allowed to enter universities. He wanted me to look it over because I am an educated woman, presumably one of the beneficiaries of this brilliant new amendment. He is also currently in court, fighting every member of the court for the sake of women everywhere. I am beyond willing to proofread this for him, Emmett, you now how badly I want women to be able to go to school like men can."

He finished skimming over the proposal and handed it to her. "I see."

"You slander my husband, and all you come up with when you are disproved is I see?" she asked, eyebrows raised.

He sighed. "I apologise. I should not have slandered your husband."

"Good," she replied, finally satisfied. "Now, seeing as your meeting overran by a good half hour, I am absolutely ravenous. Shall we eat?"

"Please, let's."

***

"WITH ALL DUE RESPECT, BROTHER, THE NOTION OF WOMEN STUDYING IN higher education sounds rather ludicrous to me," Frederick said. "The place of a woman is in the home. It has always been so. It says so in the Bible...we must abide by the word of God."

"I agree," the King said. "The place of a woman is in the home. Thank you, Frederick."

"You are ludicrous," Alexander shot back, never having spoken with a more spiteful tone in his life. "I challenge you to say that to Mother's face, Father – tell her tonight, at dinner so that all five of your children may bear witness, that the place of a woman is in the home."

"Now you are being daft, child, our private life has nothing to do with—"

"It has everything to do with this amendment! Any man with an ounce of genuine love for a woman would—"

"I will not stand for you insulting me thusly in my own court, Alexander, either cease your shameful behaviour or leave."

"Maybe I will," he snapped, standing from his chair. Before he took his leave from the room, he said, this time to Frederick, "You disappoint me, brother. Sorely."

Once the door had shut behind him, the King spoke again. "Very well, we may move on. I do apologise for Alexander's poor conduct. Are there any other issues that anyone would like to raise?"

There was only silence to be heard, and Andrew nodded. "Then you are dis—"

"Wait, Father—!" A voice cried out, and it shocked everyone in the room; for Javier St James had never once spoken in court. He had always been one to let his disinterest show, very plainly. It was well known by one and all that he had never paid attention in their meetings.

And now he stood, with as much conviction as his eldest brother had just a moment ago. "My lords, I beseech you consider my brother Alexander's proposition. Consider it not just as esteemed members of the court – consider it not just as men. Consider it as fathers, as brothers, as husbands. Think of your daughters, your sisters, even your wives – think of the women you know who want for nothing but knowledge."

There arises a steady hum in the room, and with it comes the King's increasing unease.

"Sit down, Javier, or leave like Alexander did – you are not to disrupt the order of the court!" he ordered.

But he could never have expected his least becoming son to stand his ground, more firmly than Alexander had. "I am not disrupting the order of the court, Father, this is a place where discussion ought to be made – not stifled by a ruler whenever he pleases it! If you might stop a policy you personally dislike from being debated, why have a court to begin with? As your humble subject, I pray you not to abuse your power, Father, however great it might be."

"Let His Highness speak, Your Majesty!" Duke Westchester cried, and was immediately followed by a chorus of support from all around the room.

Having no choice left, Andrew nodded resignedly. Javier smirked triumphantly at him, but only for a split second, before he returned his attentions to his wider audience.

"As my brother tried to tell you, my lords, before he was so rudely expelled from the room – if you have a single woman you care for, you will fight for the rights of women. My brother is married to a great lady, my sister-in-law Princess Emmeline, and she is vastly knowledgable. My brother wishes to pass this amendment for her. I am not attached to any such woman, but I have a mother – she is deeply intelligent, and knows much more than I do about the world. She was educated in her home, but if she were granted an opportunity to receive further education, I can only imagine how she might have rejoiced!—And if women everywhere should be granted such an opportunity now...well, she would also be overjoyed.

"My father deprived me of my education. As an adolescent I wished so deeply to study the sciences in Oxford or Cambridge, but His Majesty was of the opinion that I have greater duties in court. I do not dispute my obligation to our great kingdom, but I do know how it feels to crave further education and have it snatched from you.

"My lords, I have never asked anything of you. Let my sole request be this one: lend Prince Alexander your support. Women need to be educated as much as men do – the yearning for knowledge is a human feature, not one determined by gender. Please. Let us, for once, do something good for our kingdom."

***

This might be weird, but I'm really proud of Javier and how he's standing up for something he believes in. Let me know what you think about him...and about who the mystery man is!

With love,Leanne

# Chapter Twenty

------------------------------------------------

A /N Here's Chapter Twenty! (Note: This is NOT the finale! Regarding chapter count, Apollo is estimated to have thirty chapters! Artemis only had twenty, but Apollo has shorter chapters – if you haven't noticed! )

THE AMENDMENT WAS NOT PASSED IN COURT. BOTH PRINCES ALEXANDER and Javier were greatly disappointed, and shortly after receiving the news they sat, dejected, in the palace library with Princess Emmeline offering them comfort.

"Truly, I am deeply heartened by both your efforts," she said. "Thank you – thank you for trying. Pray do not be discouraged...I am sure you have convinced at least one or two lords to rally around this cause."

"I just cannot see why – I cannot understand these people," Javier cried. "Why would anyone not support such a cause? Those snobs seemed to react well to my speech, and Alexander wrote the proposal so well..."

She smiled at him, though it was slightly pained. "Perhaps you did touch them somewhat, but I am afraid most lords would never contradict your father's word. It cannot be helped – he is King, and they need to be in his favour. If he wishes to keep women out of the universities, he will."

"I do not comprehend him, either," he complained. "He loves our mother – I have seen it, he would go to the ends of the earth for her! Yet he will not support such a proposal – why?"

"He has his beliefs, Javier, and it might take a lot more than a woman he loves to change them...it frustrates me as much as it frustrates you, but it is how it is. He is how he is."

"I hate that man," he bit out. "I hate him. I wish there was something we could do to stop him from having his way – anything!"

There was a brief pause before Alexander spoke. "Perhaps...perhaps there is something."

"Alexander..." his wife cautioned warily, shooting him a look.

"Let's hear it, brother," Javier said eagerly. Then, turning to the princess, "Do not worry yourself quite yet, Emmeline. We know our limits."

"I—I have a contact in one of the universities – a professor, and one of substantial influence at that. Emmeline, if you should so desire me to, I could get you into some academic work there."

"M-me?" she sputtered. "In a university? Alexander—! I..."

"Your brother would have to go with you. Rather, you would have to go with him – should you agree to this, you will be there in order to assist him in some research I will task him with doing...but it would give you the chance to engage in academic study, consult with the professors and acquire knowledge you might otherwise find inaccessible."

"Is this something currently practiced?" she asked.

"Not to my knowledge, but given that I am Crown Prince...we could make it happen."

"I would have the chance to do research in a university," she marvelled at the thought.

"And Father would be hopping with anger," Javier added, smirking.

"Most importantly, it might pave the way for change," Alexander said. "Emmeline, if you can prove the intellectual capabilities of women to the academic community, we could see change."

"Change," she echoed, smiling. Then, "What about you, then? Will you not come with us?"

He shook his head with some sadness. "I'm afraid I have to remain in the castle, beloved; I have duties here. My father has no intention for any of us to go into academic work – we were all tutored privately, and he expects us to work in court for the rest of our lives."

"I see," she hummed. "Javier...Javier had told me about this."

He nodded, sombre. "I will, however, be able to send Earl Portsmouth in my place. He is, after all, my brother-in-law, my closest ally outside of my own blood relations – and I presume also highly-educated, yes?"

"Of course. Emmett graduated from Cambridge University with honours."

"Perfect, my love."


***


"THIS IS WONDERFUL, EMMETT," EMMELINE GUSHED. "THAT I MIGHT LIVE in a university with you, doing academic study! I never pictured such freedom in my married life!"

He smiled. "You have your husband to thank. He really does care for you."

"Indeed, Emmy, he is rather splendid," she agreed, grinning. "Of all the men I do not love, I consider myself rather lucky to have been wed to him." Seeing her brother's face fall slightly, she quickly changed the subject. "When shall we see Professor Whitman?"

"We will be on our way whenever Miss Smith is done unpacking your things and has dressed you, my dear," he said, a little loudly on purpose.

"Sorry!" came a squeal from the princess's bedroom. "My lady, your things are ready now, if you would like me to help you dress!"

She smiled as she drew herself to her feet. "I will see you in a moment, brother."

"Yes, yes, be on your way." Upon his chuckle and gentle nod, she turned and walked down the narrow hallway to her quarters. This was less than she was accustomed to, but it was very pleasant for an apartment, not a manor or a palace; and besides, the ability to devote all her time to the acquisition of knowledge previously not available to her was more than she could ever ask for.

Penelope helped her out of her travelling dress, slightly crumpled from being nestled in her brother's arms as she slept in the carriage, and dressed her in an inconspicuous navy gown with a pair of gloves to match. Her crown had been still away in her trunk. She was here as an assistant to her brother, on decree from her husband; she was not here to be seen.

Emmeline met her brother outside, who had, also, changed into a fresh set of clothes – a fine black suit, smart trousers, with a fashionable cravat. He offered her his arm, and they went together to see Professor George Whitman, the man responsible for overseeing their stay. He was a thinker and educator of great prestige, and had served as Alexander's private tutor a many years prior.

"Ah, good afternoon, Your Highness. Your Lordship." He stood from his chair and bowed courteously when they entered the room.

"Good day, Professor," Emmett greeted in return with a bow. Emmeline curtsied smilingly, but remained mute as she knew she was expected to. In the privacy of her own home and in the company of other women and the handful of men she was familiar with she was free to speak, as long as it was with measure and grace; but here she knew her place. This was not a woman's territory – a woman's place was where she socialised with other women, orchestrated happy marriages, and partook in pastimes like knitting and playing instruments. This was an establishment of men, and here, even as princess, she would stay wordless unless directly addressed.

"It is so wonderful to have you here. And I am deeply honoured to be in charge of assisting your research," the professor went on to say. "You will be exploring the correlation between education and life expectancy, yes?"

"Yes," Emmett replied. "On the behalf of my brother-in-law."

"Of course. Well, you must be wearied by your travel. We will begin tomorrow. If you have any questions, do feel free to raise them to me. Either of you."

"Thank you, Professor," Emmett said, sincere. Emmeline nodded her agreement, still smiling politely.

Whitman turned to her now, his gaze kind as it landed on her. "Your Hig hness...I would like to have you know that I am not quite as...conservative as some of the others you might find here. I wholeheartedly approve of your presence – in fact, I would not mind if you had come alone, and not to accompany your brother. I would be most obliged if you would speak freely in my presence."

"Yes – I will. Thank you, Professor," she said, releasing a breath she had not known she had been holding. "I see now why Alexander thinks so highly of you."

"We do agree on many things," he responded with a chuckle. "Very well, Your Highness; Your Lordship. It might be wise to get some rest. Might I suggest a stroll around campus? There are a number of lovely views."

"Oh, can we, Emmett?" she exclaimed.

Earl Portsmouth saw no reason to disagree.

And so they went on their way about campus, walking through the halls, examining the architecture, and admiring the flora all around. Passing students let their gazes linger on the princess, for she must have been the first woman they had seen in days. As they looked Emmett felt her hand tighten around his arm, but he could do nothing but pat her hand reassuringly, for they had done nothing wrong by her.

And then they saw a puzzling sight – another woman on university grounds; and not just any woman.

It was Lady Victoria Arden, gazing wistfully about the halls.

"Lady Victoria!" Emmett called out instinctively before his sister could stop him.

She froze briefly before turning to them with a tight smile painted over her lips and curtsying. "Oh – oh, Lord Portsmouth. Your Highness. Hello. How strange...how strange that I might see you here."

"I apologise if I frightened you, my lady," he said, earnest, offering a slight bow in return. "I should have—"

"No, no; no need for any apology, my lord."

A tense wordlessness fell over them. Neither of the Lockhart siblings knew what to say, and Victoria seemed to want to escape the situation.

"Lady Victoria, we called on your father Duke Westchester some days ago and we—we heard what your mother said to you," Emmeline finally said, breaking the awkward silence. "I...I have been rude to you. I apologise. I did not know that you...that you were not the one will ill intentions."

"I'm afraid I don't understand, Madam – I don't know what my mother could have possibly said to me that you would find worth apologising for, and I don't know what ill intentions you speak of." She pressed her lips into a thin line. "I—I am here with my father. I should find him now."

Emmeline's brow furrowed slightly. "Victoria, wait—"

But she had already turned and vanished down the hallway, with such speed that the twins might have wondered if she had been naught but a figment of their imagination.

***

BUT SHE WAS NOT. SHE HAD BEEN REAL, EVERY INCH OF HER – EMMETT knew this for a fact because he saw her after that, still in the university, this time with a book in her lap as she sat in a well-hidden corner. He had approached her, and she had, once again, appeared thoroughly rattled.

"May I sit, my lady?" he asked.

She hesitated, and for a moment he suspected she would invent some excuse and run off again; but then she nodded. "Yes, you may."

"What are you reading?" he asked, cautious, as if she were the finest bird he had ever seen, and might fly away if he was too loud or too soft or too forward or too reserved with his words.

"Nothing much, my lord. Rene Descartes."

"Ah," he said. "Well...do you...come here often?"

"I suppose you could say so, yes," she said. "My father is very concerned with this school's affairs. He donates to it, you see, quite generously."

"Duke Westchester is outstanding," he remarked.

"He is," she hummed, closing her book. "... If I am candid about this, Earl Portsmouth, which I sense I can be with you, the truth is that Papa comes often so that I might sit and read books from the library."

"He must love you dearly," Emmett observed. "If he would take such trouble so frequently just so that you might have a few hours to do something you love."

"Indeed." She smiled at him then, and it was genuine.

***

There were a few major developments in this chapter! Let me know what you think about it / what you think is going to happen! (Hint: Stuff gets exciting real soon.) x Leanne

# Chapter Twenty-One

HE SAW HER AFTER THAT, ALWAYS AT DIFFERENT PLACES ON CAMPUS, ON different days and times, but always reading. She read in the library in the morning; in the quieter hallways in the afternoon; in the gardens in the evening. Every time he saw her she would have a different book in hand; more and more she seemed to tolerate him, and she grew less anxious in his presence. Nonetheless, every time they parted, she would request that he did not speak of their meetings to his sister.

"I fear that she will misunderstand," she had explained to him, wringing her hands. "I'm afraid she thinks I still hope to marry you. Back when I did hope for such a thing, she made it very clear that she would not have me as a sister."

And he understood, for he knew that Emmeline had never been very kind to the Arden girl. For his undying loyalty toward his twin sister, he knew just how bitingly cold and shockingly vicious she could be if she saw someone as a threat to her loved ones. Therefore he knew how Emmeline might react, despite the apology she had already offered, if she found out that he was seeing her.

So the days passed with the princess never knowing of their encounters, and Lady Victoria would let him sit with her longer, and talk to her longer, and he came to learn about her for who she was—he learned of the beauty of her mind, he learned of her passions (none of which, it turned out, involved in the slightest socialising, drawing, painting, or playing the pianoforte), and he learned of her family. Her father she loved dearly; her sisters she felt the need to be a good example for; and her mother she sometimes felt threatened by.

She confessed this last detail quietly to him, and only on their tenth meeting. She said it thusly, with hands, he noticed, that were slightly trembling:

"Mother, she...she has great plans for me. I am her oldest daughter, and there, naturally, are expectations that she would hold for me. I do love her dearly, and I want more than anything to do her proud, but sometimes—sometimes she says things...things to frighten me, force me into submission, and it...it can be difficult."

"I understand," he replied, gentle. "I... My sister and I heard some things she said to you the other day. By accident, of course, we were only passing by." He swallowed, searching for the right words to say. "Her Grace—she was harsh on you, my lady, you must not let it upset you too greatly."

"I know," she said sombrely. "Your sister, Her Royal Highness...she mentioned it that day. When I saw the you in the hallway."

"I remember that occasion." He hesitated briefly.

Then, "How do you feel about my sister, Lady Victoria?"

She shrugged with a resigned smile. "I will admit that I have no credible opinion of her, my lord; I only know of her what my mother has told me, and the little I have seen of her." She stopped there, but Emmett's expectant gaze prompted her to reveal more. "Mother... My mother says she is black-hearted and power-hungry. And she was unkind to me before, but she has apologised for it, quite sincerely if I read her correctly; and thinking on it, anyway, she has never made any attack on my character, nor did she ever say anything particularly unreasonable or cruel. She only warned me away from you after I, indirectly, confessed that I did not love you as she expected me to."

She paused. "I suppose that only makes her a dutiful sister."

"Do you dislike her?"

"I have no reason to, my lord."

"Sometimes one does not require a reason to dislike someone else."

She thought this over, carefully, and it was quite some time before she said anything at all. "No," she answered slowly, "no, I do not believe I do."

"Good," he said, letting out a breath.

She chuckled. "Why do you sound so relieved, Earl Portsmouth?—Even if I detested Her Highness with all my heart, I could never act upon it. It would be treason...and Prince Alexander would have my head."

"I value your opinion, my lady," he replied.

"Well," she said, standing then, smoothing out imaginary creases in her skirt, "perhaps you should not. No one really does, with the exception of my father, of course; but he is different."

"Lady Victoria, I..."

"I appreciate your friendship, Earl Portsmouth, and with all my heart; but I pray you remember that my deepest affections belong to another. I only remind you because you are a good man, Your Lordship... I would never like to mislead you." Her voice held some regret, but her tone was firm. She paused. "My lord—I agreed to meet Papa by the gates, and I shall be late if I do not begin on my way now."

He nodded. "Of course, my lady. Take care."

"I will. Thank you." She smiled at him, but just barely, before she turned and walked away from him.

She was nothing but a friend to him, he knew it.

But still he felt something in his heart sink.

***

"OH! HOW FASCINATING, PROFESSOR, THANK YOU. I NEVER DID KNOW about that," Emmeline exclaimed, sitting with Professor Whitman in his office and going over some of Emmett's findings. "I understand now."

"Very good, Your Highness," he said, smiling kindly at her. "So now we can see that there is a clear correlation between educational attainment and life expectancy – not causation, as you now know – and it might now perhaps be wise to explore how can make education more accessible for all."

"Perhaps by looking into the greatest barriers to education?"

"Excellent, Madam." Approval shone in his eyes. "I would suggest that His Lordship – and yourself, of course – go about creating questions now."

"Yes. Thank you for your help, Professor Whitman," she replied, grinning. "I will relay this to my brother. He has been curiously absent lately... Well, either way, I shall be on my way now."

When she returned to the apartment he was gazing out their sitting room window, deep in thought. He turned to look at her when the door clicked shut, smiling slightly.

"Where did you go?" he asked.

"Why, talking with Professor Whitman. There is much more to be done – here. I took notes." She handed him a document, which he accepted with a word of thanks. "Where did you go?"

"I...I bumped into an old friend."

"You must have been bumping into him a lot, then."

"What?—No, I only just saw...saw him today." He rubbed the back of his neck.

Her eyes narrowed immediately. "Are you hiding something from me, Emmett? I thought we agreed—"

"No," he interrupted. "No, nothing. Of course not. I'll read this file in my bedroom."

And he vanished down the hall faster than she could say liar.

***

IT WAS NEARLY MIDNIGHT WHEN VICTORIA ARDEN SLIPPED INTO HIS chambers, her face partly hidden with a heavy cloak. She had ridden here on horseback, the way she always did, her identity hidden by the shadow of night. The palace guards already knew of this mysterious nighttime visitor, although they never knew her name.

"What are you doing here?" he asked, his voice cold. Well, it always was these days, but on this moonlit night he seemed more glacial than usual. There was a pang in her heart as she remembered happier times...once, seemingly far too long ago, there was a time when he would have been glad to see her.

"I came to see you, of course."

He turned his back to her. "I have no need for your company tonight."

"Have you thought about what I said?" she asked. In sooth they both knew that she was really pleading with him to say yes, but still she forced herself to maintain her composure for the sake of decorum and dignity, the only sign of her emotional state being the way her words were quiet and quivering.

"Yes," he said, and her heart lifted momentarily, "and the answer is no."

"But—" she cried, her desperation finally breaking down her restraint.

He sighed, but it sounded more irritated than regretful. "I pray you do not throw another one of your fits at me, Victoria; truly, you need not see me any longer if my decision infuriates you so. You are not as indispensable to me as I might be to you."

"But you cannot scorn me now! It is too late... What if...what if I am already with child?" she asked, eyes shimmering in the dim candlelight.

"If you find out that you are indeed with child, you may write me, and I will send a doctor and finance you adequately," he replied, unruffled. "Now go – leave me in peace. These tantrums are rather unbecoming of you, Lady Victoria."

She stayed put. "And how will I answer to my parents? How will I tell them that I have lain with a man I did not marry?—My mother would have my head, and Papa would be so ashamed!"

"Do not tell them, then, and marry someone else. You are beautiful and affluent, with no shortage of suitors; and your parents would never know the difference!"

"I pray you do not make a mockery of them," she said, her voice taking on an edge now as she realised that the man she loved so dearly might not love her back. "Mother will know. She always knows."

"Not if you do not tell her, Victoria," he disagreed, sighing. "Please, now will you not leave me be? You know I will have you forcefully removed if you force my hand."

"You cannot shun me, Javier, I refuse to let you!" she insisted, hackles raising. "You have already claimed me as your own!"

"I do not objectify women as you seem to, my lady, I never did claim you as you say," he replied, "but if you truly are my property, I may dispose of you as I please."

"The gall of you to say that you do not objectify women! You treat me like an object, like I can be tossed aside without repercussion. Did I mean nothing to you?—Answer me this, whatever was I to you?"

She saw something flash in his eyes as he turned abruptly to her. "I loved you, Victoria, I never treated you as an object!"

For a moment her heart stopped. I loved you.

"You were fascinating," the third-born prince went on, "a woman so invested in the academics! It might pain you to know that I once planned to be wed to you – I was simply waiting, for once you brought it up, I was to agree to it and everything would be perfect, you and I, we would have been so happy—!" Something caught in his throat then, so he cleared it, and he returned to his icy self. "But then you turned out to be like all the rest, and I lost interest. I decided I would not marry, not you, not anyone, not ever. Alexander was right when he said it years ago – true love is not real. And you... Like I said to you the last time you saw me – you are far too much for me. Far too scheming, far too complicated, far too difficult to understand...far too difficult to love."

"What do you mean, Javier, I—"

"Oh, save me this ridiculousness. Your pursuits of Earl Portsmouth...of my own brother – Frederick! I suppose, then, you are only after the money and power every other woman in pursuit of a man is? And I am your new target, now that my eldest brother and my sister-in-law have chased you away from them both? The real question here, Victoria, is what did I mean to you?—A ticket to the crown, perhaps?"

"I would never make use of you thusly, Javier...I love you," she pleaded.

"You cannot promise me that." He swallowed. "You cannot promise me anything. I loved you, and being with you was a risk that I took trusting in our future together...but now it is no more, and continuing to see you will only tarnish my reputation if I am found out."

He turned away from her once again, looking out his window and into the night. "Besides...the sight of you breaks my heart. So please spare me. Leave me be."

***

A/N Who actually already knew that Victoria's secret lover was Javier? If you didn't guess right, who did you think it was? And what are your thoughts on Javier and Victoria now? Let me know in the comments and don't forget to vote!!! It really means a lot :") See you next week! x Leanne

# Chapter Twenty-Two

A/N Words cannot describe how sorry I am. I've just had this really important exam and banged this out as quickly as I could after. Unfortunately the insane amount of plot development in this chapter made it slightly harder to write and it took me a few days :d Either way, here's Chapter Twenty-Two, piping hot, fresh from the oven and full of drama! (Trust me...this is the most dramatic the story has ever been. I hope that makes up for the lateness.)

A MONTH HAD PASSED IN THE BLINK OF AN EYE, AND WITH THAT THE Lockhart twins' residence in the university had drawn to a close. In Emmeline's opinion it was all too soon, but there was little work left to do, and whatever was left could be completed outside of campus.

The larger reason for having to return to her home in St James' Palace, however, was a large party that the Queen was about to throw, the grandest soiree of the year. It was in honour of her wedding anniversary with King Andrew – and this year was a celebration of their thirtieth, meaning that it would be the most extravagant one yet.

Presently there was an hour left until Emmeline was due to make her appearance in the royal ballroom, and Penelope was preparing her for the event. As she helped put on the pastel pink lace dress, she asked, "Are you looking forward to the dance, my lady?"

"I would rather be researching with Emmett in the university," the princess answered, somewhat sullenly. "Now that I have tasted study...dancing feels like a waste of my time."

She laughed. "Take it as a moment of rest from academia, my lady, after weeks of research you would surely enjoy a night of dancing and music?"

Emmeline considered this for a moment before nodding with a light smile. "You are quite right, Penny, I think I might enjoy letting loose for just a night. I have had much too much on my mind for much too long."

"Well, there you have it," the lady-in-waiting said, grinning. "His Highness will come to walk you to the ballroom shortly, my lady, and he will be pleased. You look beautiful."

She was right. Alexander was positively beaming as she took his arm, and he commented as charmingly as always, "Why, all the lords shall been green with envy, for I will have the most beautiful woman in the room on my arm tonight."

"They would envy you enough for being crown prince," she said with a roll of her eyes. "Besides, the limelight tonight belongs to your mother. Make sure that no one causes a scene, would you?—I will, of course, also be on the lookout."

"Of course," he said. "Anything for my wife."

"You're such a charmer." She laughed. "But I am not jesting, Alexander. Your mother has been dreaming of tonight for months now, and she even called me home from my study so that the whole family would be in attendance – it means a lot to her, and it is paramount that the party is no less than perfect."

"Pray do not worry yourself," he said, patting her hand reassuringly. "I promise I will be vigilant tonight to make sure that no one will ruin this for Mother. Besides, what could possibly go wrong?"

She sighed. "I don't know. I just have a feeling...And that is what frightens me most of all."

***

IT WOULD SEEM AS IF EMMELINE'S CONCERN HAD BEEN FOR NAUGHT, FOR the party was going without a hitch. The music was lively, the food was more delectable than the princess had ever tasted it, and guests – all dressed to the nines – were enjoying themselves immensely.

Presently she stood with her brother and father, discussing the research the twins had done in the past many days. William Lockhart was listening, intrigued, as Emmeline outlined the parameters of their study and the results they were in the midst of analysing. Emmett contributed to the discussion occasionally, often offering details about how pleased Professor Whitman had been with Emmeline's work.

The four royal brothers stood talking on the mezzanine floor where their thrones were situated, all of them gazing over the party with watchful eyes as the princess had requested her husband do. Sarah and Andrew danced in the middle of the ballroom, without a hint of question the couple drawing the most attention in the room. Not less than half of partygoers were looking on as they waltzed and talking of how fortunate they were to have found a truly blissful marriage, and to remain so in love even in their old age. The Queen was laughing at something her husband had said, and the King smiled lovingly down upon his wife.

"Mother seems rather happy," Alexander commented.

"Indeed. They both do," Frederick agreed. "I'm glad they are enjoying themselves. They might not have been the most attentive of parents growing up, but I do suppose that there are prices to pay for royalty."

The older prince did not give an answer. He paused, spying a female figure scaling the stairs before them. He squinted at her, before finally identifying a few features he knew – dark brown locks, squared shoulders, a certain determination in her gait...

"Is that Lady Victoria Arden?—I did think she would leave us alone after my last exchange with her."

Frederick paled visibly. "Oh, dear Lord. Excuse me, brothers, I would like to temporarily retire to the library."

"I will accompany you," Javier offered, and the two ducked through a service door to flee the scene. Alexander and Lionel exchanged a glance, but could not escape themselves, for Victoria Arden was already curtsying to them.

"Good evening, Your Royal Highnesses," she greeted.

They bowed in return.

"Good evening, Lady Victoria," Alexander said. "May I assist you with anything?"

"I was actually looking for Prince—"

"I'm afraid Frederick is currently unavailable," he said. "He is...dancing."

"And Prince Javier, Your Highness?"

He furrowed his brow. "What business do you have with him? As far as I am aware, you have never met. Pray correct me if I am mistaken?"

She seemed to grow anxious, wringing her hands. "I...No, Sir, you are not mistaken. But I—please, I need to see him!"

"You are hiding something from me, my lady," he replied, unruffled and unyielding. "What is it?"

"Nothing. I—Please, I just need to see him."

"Why?" His tone grew firmer now, more pressing.

"I—I can't tell you."

"In the name of the Crown, Lady Victoria, I compel you to answer my question!"

She paled instantly, and sputtered, "Ex-Excuse me, Your Highness. I...I do not feel well." She turned, running down the steps and out of the ballroom, leaving behind two very confused princes.

Minutes later, the princess, on her way to her study to collect a document to show to her father, was even more bewildered to find her in a hallway not far outside the ballroom, emptying the contents of her stomach on the polished floor.

"Oh, my word, Lady Victoria!" she exclaimed. Then, turning to her lady in waiting beside her, "Quickly, Penny, fetch her a bucket and some warm water, and have a maid come by to clean this up."

She obliged, scampering off with a brief curtsy, and Emmeline went to Victoria's side. She held the sick woman's chocolate locks back as she continued to heave and retch, and tried to ignore the stench that threatened to upset her own stomach. Penelope returned soon enough with the items she had been told to bring, as well as with a slightly flustered maid in tow, dragging along another bucket full of soapy water a rag.

"Let me attend to her, my lady," the younger girl said to the princess, before holding the bucket under Victoria's mouth. When Victoria took the bucket from her, she moved on to hold back her hair as Emmeline had been doing not too long ago, rubbing her back soothingly.

"I apologise, Princess," Victoria croaked the moment she was able to do so. "Sincerely. For soiling the hallway."

"No, no, Lady Victoria, this is no time for such talk. Come, have some water, you must have lost a lot of it—Penelope?"

Doing as she was bid, the lady in waiting brought the warm water to Victoria's lips. She drank gratefully, and when she had drained the cup she smiled sheepishly at Emmeline. "Thank you, Your Highness."

"Not a problem, Lady Victoria.—I hope the food did not upset your stomach?"

"No, no, Madam, certainly not; for I have not yet had a bite of it since I arrived. If I am honest...I have been sick for a while now. It always happens in the evenings. I...I should see a doctor, I know, but I am scared..."

"Fear of illness is never a reason to avoid seeing a physician," Emmeline chided in a big-sisterly fashion. "Come, now I will show you to a room. I will send for a maid to bathe you and dress you in a clean gown, and you may rest while I call you a doctor. Is that all right with you?"

Victoria struggled to speak, her eyes turning slightly red. The princess's eyebrows raised in alarm. "Have I upset you?—What did I say that—"

"No, no, Madam, you have said nothing wrong," she replied quiveringly, smiling through her sniffles. "It is only that I have done nothing to deserve such kindness from you. I was so rude to you when we first met...I heard things about you, you know, but I should not have believed them. I thought ill of you for so long...and when you apologised at the university I lacked the character to accept it and make peace. I have wronged you, and still you are so kind to me – I must apologise."

Emmeline only smiled. "I bear no resentment toward you, Lady Victoria – you once posed a threat to my brother's happiness, but now that you no longer do I have no more cause to dislike you. Now you must rest. Come with me."

***

EVERYONE WAS GATHERED AROUND THE DOCTOR, SOME MORE ANXIOUS than others, as Emmeline asked how Lady Victoria was – Prince Alexander, the Dukes Mayfair and Westchester and Duchess Georgeanne; Emmett was present, in a far corner of the room, and, of course, the princess stood in the middle of the lot. Victoria lay in the bed beside them, less spirited than usual but far more energetic than she had been when Emmeline left her to recover.

"Will she be all right?" she asked worriedly, "She tells me she has been unwell for some days now."

"She is not unwell, Your Royal Highness," the royal physician said with a broad grin. "In fact, I would say quite the opposite."

"What, is her body purging her of toxins? Under what scenario is vomiting a symptom of something desirable, I pray you not speak in riddles!" Emmeline exclaimed, her exasperation obvious.

"I apologise, Madam, I will be direct." He paused, and the room was so quiet one could hear a pin drop.

"You see, Lady Victoria Arden is with child."

"What?" There was a collective gasp.

"That is not possible, doctor, my daughter is pure as pure can be!" Georgeanne Arden screeched. "A baby takes a man and a woman, and she has most definitely never laid with a man!" She swung around to face her daughter, eyes wide, brow creased sternly. "Have you?"

The girl was quaking at this point, eyes wide as saucers. "I...Mother, I..."

"Answer me, Victoria!"

"I'm sorry..." She began to weep now, and Emmeline felt a pang in her heart as she watched disaster unfold. Poor thing...But she had to take responsibility for the choices she had made.

"Whose child is it?" Georgeanne demanded, hysterical. "Who is the father, I demand to know!"

"He will not have me, Mother, he has left me already," she sobbed. "He—He says I do not love him, he saw me with Prince Frederick and assumed...I begged him, but he will not grant me his audience, not at all, I—I am so sorry, Mother!"

"And who is this he, Victoria?" Duke Westchester spoke now. "I swear—I will kill him myself if he will not take responsibility for his child!"

"Father, I cannot...I love him, I—please!"

"Victoria, his name!" His voice was hard and unforgiving, and though his ire was not meant for his daughter his tone caused her to shake more violently yet.

"I cannot..."

Georgeanne was shrieking again, daggers in her eyes. "I swear to God, I am going to burn all your things and make you suf—"

"The child is mine!"

***

I wonder who made that last shocking announcement at the end. Any guesses? As usual, please please please leave your lovely comments and votes behind! Once again I apologise for this update being so late :(

# Chapter Twenty-Three

A/N Hey guys!!! Yay for semi-punctual updates? Sorry this is a day or so late! I hope you enjoy this one – no cliffhanger this time Before I jump into the chapter, though, I'd like to take a moment to say a huge THANK YOU for 1k reads on Apollo and 6k reads on Artemis! It's honestly crazy that people read this stuff. I'm super honoured and I hope you guys enjoy reading the rest of the story as I enjoy writing it! x Leanne

EMMETT LOCKHART AND VICTORIA ARDEN SAT IN SILENCE, NEITHER SURE of what to say to the other.

He closed his eyes and took a breath. He could still feel the sting of his sister's palm meeting his face; but more than that he could feel, acutely, the pain she had left in his heart. "How could you?" she'd spat at him with tears brimming in her eyes; then she'd fled the room with Prince Alexander running after her, and his heart had shattered. He hadn't meant to upset her so...he hadn't meant to do anything, really, he hadn't been thinking very much at all as he declared that the child was his.

Georgeanne Arden had, of course, demanded that he take responsibility for his supposed child. He agreed to marry Victoria within the month.

The look of disappointment on his father's face had crushed him. Duke Westchester had seemed equally dismayed. He'd responded to William's profuse apologies with a resigned smile, saying that this was, in a way, what they'd wanted all along; he only wished that his daughter would have been more discerning and honest. William said the same of his son. Both men had then left the room, looking rather heavyhearted, with the duchess in tow.

"I'm sorry," Emmett blurted out presently.

"You were trying to save my skin," she said, wiping the silent tears off her cheeks. Everyone hated her now, she knew it. Her father had looked particularly disconcerted as he spoke with Duke Mayfair, and perhaps it was not her mother's fury that upset her most but the sadness she had spied in her beloved Papa's eyes. "You made a sacrifice for me. I should be thanking you."

There was a yet another drawn-out silence between them before he spoke again, his question spoken quietly but jarring to both their ears.

"Who is the father?"

She sighed. "I suppose I must tell you now, mustn't I?"

"It would be preferable to know whose child I am taking responsibility for, yes." He had meant to jest, to lighten the mood for both their sakes, but the words left his mouth sad and lifeless, and sounded like more of a lament than anything.

"The baby...It is Prince Javier's," she admitted softly. She was almost ashamed to say his name, for more reasons than one.

"You love him." It was more of a statement than anything; she had mentioned her lover to him before, not by name, but she had spoken of her affections for him once, during one of their campus conversations.

She confirmed it anyway – they both needed to hear it come from her mouth.

"Yes."

"You said he will not see you."

"No, he will not. He had a broken heart already, and now I have broken it beyond repair...and my baby will pay the price." She swallowed. "I did not know about the child yet when I last spoke to him, but he said that, should there be one, he would finance it. That I would have use of the palace doctors."

"I suppose it may at least be said that he is better than some men." He shook his head sadly. "I really am sorry, Lady Victoria, for everything that has happened to you."

"You can be blamed for none of it," she said. "It is quite the opposite, actually. I...I only fail to understand why you would do such a thing for me. The baby, it is not yours...You did not have to say it was. Now you will have to face my parents, and your sister is clearly upset with you...None of this is your responsibility."

"To be frank, my lady, I do not understand either," he said. "I suppose I care for you more than I would otherwise admit."

She paused, unsure of how to answer him. Was that a proclamation of love? Or was he only referring to our friendship? Finally, she said, "It is not too late to reverse the damage. We could tell everyone the truth."

He considered this. "We could talk to my sister about it. I need to apologise and tell her the truth, I could not have her hate me again...But, more importantly, she has been able to befriend Prince Javier. She might be able to help you."

"Oh, she would never help me," she replied, wearing a sad smile. "She detests me now; I am no imbecile, I saw it in her eyes. She forgave me once, and I betrayed her again."

"Regardless of your past disagreements, and whatever misunderstanding you currently have, she will always stand up for another woman. It is in her nature to protect those who are wrongfully harmed – she could not turn you down without breaching her guiding principles."

"Do you...Do you really think so?" she asked, suddenly sounding hopeful. "She would—she could help me?"

"I do," he said, smiling. "I really do."

***

"EMMELINE?" ALEXANDER GREETED GENTLY AS HE STEPPED GINGERLY into her bedroom. She sat staring stoically out a window and into the gardens below, her back to him, but he still caught a glimpse of the way she rushed to conceal her handkerchief under her skirts as she heard him enter the room.

"Please come outside. It's been hours," he said softly. "I worry for you."

"I am quite all right here by myself," she replied. "I would rather like to be alone now...it is barely after noon, and it has been such a long day already."

There was a pause. "Your brother and Lady Victoria Arden are asking to see you. I have directed them to your study."

"I will not grant them my audience."

"Emmeline, beloved..."

"He promised me there would be no more secrets, Alexander, he lied, he keeps lying to me!" she cried. Then, quietly, "I will not see him."

He sighed, coming to sit beside her. "You know that I will always take your side in arguments such as this one – I am your husband, not Emmett's after all –, but you are letting your emotions blind you...the same way my father does, and the same way your brother did before. You are outstanding for your rationality...pray do not take that away from yourself."

She looked at him then, an unidentifiable emotion burning in her eyes. "Is there something you know that I do not?"

"No," he said, "but they did say that there is something crucial that you must be made aware of. In my opinion, it might be worth hearing."

She was silent for a long while, but when he started growing uneasy, she spoke again.

"Very well," she said. "I suppose will hear it."

His lips stretched into a smile. "May I walk you to them?"

She nodded, and they stood together. When they arrived at the door of her study, he pushed it open for her, and she stepped in alone.

"Emmeline." He brother stood immediately when she entered. "You could not fathom how relieved I am to see you."

"I only came for Alexander's sake," she replied icily. "I was reluctant, but he insisted that I grant you my audience."

"Then I am indebted to him forever," he said. "For Emmeline, you must know that the child is not mine."

"Excuse me?"

"It is true. Lord Portsmouth and I have not... We have not had any such relationships," Victoria confirmed.

"Whose, then, is it?" she asked sharply, eyes narrowed at the girl.

"It...It is Prince Javier's."

"What?" she yelped.

"Yes." Victoria cast her eyes toward the ground.

"Then why did you claim otherwise?" Emmeline demanded, turning to her brother now. "Why would you do such a thing?"

"Her mother was threatening her," he said. "I could not leave her in the lurch—"

"And why not?" she interrupted sharply. "There is a difference from being kind and being suicidal, Emmett, you took responsibility for impregnating a duke's eldest daughter! You know, I wish you would think things through for once!"

"Well, maybe it wasn't about being kind, Emmeline, maybe I love her!"

"What?" the princess shrieked. Beside her Victoria stiffened visibly.

"I love you," he said, turning to look the brown-haired girl in the eye. "We have different upbringings and perhaps several different opinions, but I think you are beautiful in every sense of the word."

She was flabbergasted, her eyes flitting from the earl to his sister and back to him again. "I... Your Lordship, I..." she stuttered, at a clear loss for words.

Before she could form a sentence, though, Emmeline spoke again, cold as stone. "Get out of my study. Both of you."

"Emmeline..."

"Now!" she snapped. They complied; and once they had left the room, she rang for Penelope to enter, and when the lady in waiting rushed into the room to attend to her, she sent for Prince Javier.

"I want to see him. Now." She looked absolutely thunderous as she said this, her green eyes a shade darker than they usually were.

"Are you sure, my lady? I—"

"I said now!"

"Very well." She said these words with some regretfulness showing in her tone; yet she was, at the end of the day, but a lady in waiting and so she spoke them obediently as she curtsied, before leaving in search of the younger prince.

In the meantime Emmeline stewed in her study, growing more livid by the minute. The audacity of him, to refuse to be a man and care for his own child and the woman who should be his wife – and now her brother would bear the responsibility that he was too much of a coward to take up! She knew that he was troubled, and she did have a fair amount of sympathy for him, but it was no excuse to go around destroying lives! She, after all, had also been deprived of parents at a young age, her father just as distant to her as his had been to him; but it certainly did not mean that she would go around making poor decisions and refusing to face the music for them.

Javier stepped into her study looking rather jovial, but his face fell instantly when he saw her sitting unsmilingly at her desk with better posture than usual.

"Emmeline," he greeted cautiously. "You sent for me."

"Ah, Javier. Have a seat."

He sat across the desk from her, and waited for her to speak. It seemed like an eternity before she did, though in truth she only paused for a brief moment.

"Have you heard?" she asked, her tone eerily measured.

His brow crumpled slightly, and he spoke warily. "Is there something that I should have heard of?"

"Only that Victoria Arden is with child," she said.

"She's...what?"

"Pregnant. With my brother's child." His eyes widened considerably at this; in contrast, her composure only told him that there was more to what she was saying; that she knew more than what she was saying. "He told me he wasn't seeing her anymore. Can you believe him?—How many times must he lie to me?"

"I... Perhaps you should speak to him about this."

She ignored him. "If you ask me, what's even more ridiculous is that he initially refused to take responsibility for the child! Victoria Arden said it herself – he got jealous when he saw her with Frederick, and refused to see her ever again."

"I...I'm not sure how I should react, Emmeline, he is your brother after all..."

"You may answer me this simple question – do you not think it is slightly strange, though, that he refused to see Lady Victoria but was in the room with us when the doctor was explaining her condition? Why would he suddenly choose to admit that the child is his? Or, at least, that she, who so desperately wanted to see him, had no reaction at all to him standing in the corner?" She cocked an eyebrow, daring him to answer.

"I..."

"Truthfully, please, Javier; yes or no?"

"No," he said, "because Lady Victoria was keeping a secret."

"Whose exactly?"

He sighed. "Emmeline, enough of this game. We both know you that you know that it is mine."

"The secret, or the baby?"

"Both."

She narrowed her eyes at him. "So how dare you sit in front of me, so free of worry, when my brother is taking the blame for your mistakes – for your child?"

"My mistakes? No – Victoria failed me. She must take responsibility for what she has done."

"And my brother? Must he, then, face the consequences for your poor broken heart?" Her volume was rising now.

"Your brother made a choice when he said that the child was his," Javier said. "I cannot hear his thoughts. He made a decision that I cannot explain, and that I am not accountable for." He paused. "Have you ever considered, Sister, that perhaps what Earl Portsmouth wants does not coincide with what you want for him?"

Well, maybe it wasn't about being kind, Emmeline, maybe I love her! She could hear Emmett's voice again, the words that had filled her with so much anger. Victoria was no good for him, and this child was no good for him, and he could not marry her and father a child that was never even his...he couldn't!

"How dare you shirk responsibility for your child by saying it is what Emmett wants, how dare you let him ruin himself for your own selfishness!" she roared. "He is my brother, Javier, I will not let him marry a woman as vicious and scheming as her and father a child which is not his because of your foolishness!"

"He has presented himself as the father," the prince said adamantly. "He has made his will clear. I will not fight him for the child...and I will most certainly not fight him for Victoria. It pains me to see her."

"I felt sorry for you, you know," she said, bitter. "I was willing to overlook your rudeness because I empathised with your childhood. But now I see you for who you really are – a child who never really grew up, so self-centred and shameless. Your child...Your child should be glad that it will never call you 'Father'."

And she stood. "Consider this, if you would; and should you ever choose to be a man about this and face your own consequences, you may inform me duly."

She stalked out of the room, and he buried his face in his hands.

He knew what her interests were in this argument, and he knew that she was hardly an objective person in this matter; but in her words he heard truth, and it tore him in two.

***

# Chapter Twenty-Four

A /N Hello everyone! Sorry that this update is just a little late, but here it is! Fair warning – the next two might be fairly tardy, since I have a bunch of tests coming up >< Well, I won't hold you back from this one any longer; enjoy!

"MY LORD—LADY VICTORIA?" PENELOPE SMITH GREETED AS SHE STEPPED into the guest room Emmeline had allowed Victoria Arden to borrow. Emmett had chosen to stay overnight in the palace as well, in a separate room of course, hoping against hope that his physical presence on the castle grounds would increase his chances of gaining his sister's forgiveness.

"I hope I am not interrupting a conversation of any importance?"

"No, no, Miss Smith, it is wonderful to see you," Emmett answered hurriedly, standing immediately. "Did my sister send word?—Is she all right?"

"I am here in her stead," she replied. "Her Highness sent you this letter."

He accepted the envelope from her, and she curtsied and left.

"What does it say?" Victoria asked, her voice equal parts anxious and eager. She stood in front of him as he broke the wax seal open and pulled the letter out. "Read it aloud."

Emmett

I have spoken with Prince Javier about Victoria Arden and her baby. He admitted to being the child's father, but he has not yet agreed to take responsibility (as you so valiantly have). He will not, as he says, 'fight you for it'.

I would like to make it clear that I am not in support of your decisions. Prince Javier raised a point I think is valid, that perhaps what I want for you differs from what you want for yourself; but I would like to remind you that what you think is best for yourself has previously shown to be most disastrous. Heaven knows what strange motivations you now have for claiming to love that woman! As I have made known I bear no resentment toward her, but from what I know of her I can safely say that the two of you are completely incompatible. I disapprove of your prospective matrimony wholeheartedly.

At the present moment the very sight of you frays my nerves, and I would not like to see you about this (or about anything at all). If you must have counsel you should speak to Father about this, and speak to him truthfully. You have been successful in breaking his heart once again, and I would like you to make the truth known to him. He is young no longer, he cannot take so much heartache.

You have to start thinking with your head and not your impulses, Emmett, this bad habit of yours has caused this family far too much grief.

With extreme disappointment, Emmeline

He folded the letter up, slid it back into the envelope and placed it in his breast pocket. He did not comment further, choosing instead simply to sit down again in his armchair.

"I'm sorry I have caused you so much trouble, my lord," Victoria said quietly.

"This is not your fault," he said, sighing. "My sister is right. I am far too rash, and I have brought the ones I love pains because of it."

"...Will you tell His Grace?"

"Yes," he said, "I have no choice. As Emmeline pointed out, none of this is fair to him." Observing the uneasy look that spread across her face, he chuckled, but there was no cheer in it. "Fret not. He can keep a secret."

"I have no doubt about that, but...my father is one of his dearest friends."

He smiled tiredly. "He will not divulge any information that we wish him not to, Lady Victoria, I promise. If it helps ease your mind, I will not tell him who the true father is."

And so he returned to Wellington House that afternoon, and sat down for tea with his father. William was more distant than usual, slightly reminiscent, in fact, of how he had behaved toward his children before they had been rid of their misunderstandings, but Emmett could not fault him for it at all. All this was, after all, yet another result of his rash behaviour.

"Father," he said, "there is something I must say to you."

The greying duke shook his head slightly as he buttered a scone. "I require no apology, Emmett. I am not angry, only disappointed, and I'm afraid nothing you say could ease that now."

"You don't understand, Father. The child is not mine."

Slowly, then, Duke Mayfair looked up at him; and slower yet he asked, "What did you just say?"

"The child is not mine," the earl repeated, although he knew that his father had heard him loud and clear. "I only said so because Lady Victoria was under so much fire from her mother...I could not stand to let her bear that alone."

He paused to consider this before speaking again. "And why was that?"

"I love her, Father."

William nodded, leaning back in his chair. "I see." Then, "And what does your sister make of it?"

"She opposes it vehemently," he replied with a resigned chuckle. "I know she is only acting in my interests – she thinks Victoria incompatible with me, but I have seen sides of her that Emmeline has not."

William nodded again, gazing wordlessly out the window opposite his seat.

"Father... Do you think I made the right decision?" Emmett asked after many moments, uneasy.

He sighed. "It depends."

"On?"

"If Lady Victoria will love you back. If she will, then your sister will not stand in the way of your marriage."

This struck a chord within him, and suddenly he realised his greatest mistake of all. It was not standing up for a woman he cared for, nor was it following his heart; but as Emmeline had written in her letter, he had to start thinking with his head and not his impulses.

"You love him."

"Yes."

He might love her, but her heart still belonged to Prince Javier, and he did not know how he would win it from him.

If he failed to do so, he could make yet another woman in his life whom he cared for miserable for the rest of her life. He had already done so once, to his sister, only realising his folly when the situation had veered out of his control – and he did not know if it was too late not to do it again.

***

"WE NEED TO TALK, JAVIER." SHE STOOD AT THE ENTRANCE TO HIS ROOM – he had made the mistake of leaving the door open – with her left fist clenched by her side, watching him from behind as he pulled his jacket on, bathed in the golden afternoon light as it streamed through his bedroom window.

"There is nothing to talk about, Victoria," he said impassively. "Besides, I have to go to court. I have no time for your frivolities."

She was willing to ignore the fact that he had called her child a frivolity. "We both know that you are not required there quite yet."

"We also both know that I am growing rather tired of your pestering." He was buttoning his jacket up now.

Her brow furrowed. "Javier, please. Just a moment."

"I will not be rid of you if I do not grant you some of my time, will I?" he sighed.

"No, you will not." She remained resolute, this tone of voice slightly foreign to his ears now as it came from her lips. It was her steadfastness that he had fallen in love with when they first met; yet she had spent the past few weeks begging and pleading with him. Seeing this side of her again filled him with a sense of a nostalgia. This was a woman he had loved once.

Once.

He did not love her any longer, but she still did hold a special place in his heart.

"Well, then, what do you want?"

"I want you to take responsibility for the child and marry me."

"I cannot." He shook his head. "I cannot marry a woman I do not trust. I can no longer trust you to love me, Victoria, you don't begin to fathom"—he closed his eyes and pressed three fingers to the bridge of his nose—"you do not begin to fathom how much it hurt to know that you could have married my brother – my own brother! – if not for the fact that he did not reciprocate your...sentiment."

"Could I ever make it up to you?" she asked, eyes brimming with tears. But her tone was not so much desperate this time as it was resigned, for she already knew his answer, and perhaps, she thought to herself, it was time to accept how he felt toward her – or rather, how he no longer felt.

"No...No, you could not," he said, giving her the answer she had expected. This time, though, he sounded more regretful than annoyed; and after a brief pause he even added, "I'm sorry."

"I...I understand." She swallowed. "And the child? What arrangements would you like to make for it?"

"As I said, I will finance the child, and provide it access to the palace doctors," he said. "That can likely be done without issue. It will, after all, be considered Princess Emmeline's nephew."

"And would you—? Ever like to—?..."

"No," he said, shaking his head gently. "I do not need to know the child. Raise it as Portsmouth's; as far as the child is concerned, I will only ever be an uncle to it."

"I...Very well," she replied quietly, knowing that he would not tolerate any dispute she might have over this proposal.

They were both silent for a brief moment; and then she said, "I really am sorry."

"I know."

"I still love you."

"I know." He paused. "But you must love someone else now. I am not the man for you – I should have known from the start that I was never meant to marry. Having a wife is...simply not in my fate."

When she said nothing, he continued, "Portsmouth is giving his life up for you, you know, even though he has no duty to you and even though he knows that the child is not his. He...He cares deeply for you."

"I am aware," she answered, "and I know I should be grateful."

"Well, Victoria, what he wants from you is not gratitude." He sighed, before straightening slightly. "I'm afraid must go now."

"Yes." She nodded. "You ought to be on your way to court."

"I am glad we are parting on amicable terms, Lady Victoria, and I wish you all the best." With that he offered a bow to her, a wordless bittersweet goodbye. This would be how things were between them from then on; their relationship would be that between a rebellious prince and a fine lady already taken by another man, courteous and amiable but not half as warm intimate as she wished it could be.

Remembering herself and her place before a prince to whom she was no longer special in any way, she hurried to curtsy back, and as her head was lowered politely he stepped silently past her and vanished down the hallway. She did not turn to watch as he left her; instead she drew herself to her full height and looked ahead.

It was only after the echo of his footsteps against the marble floor could no longer be heard that she allowed herself to close her eyes slowly. She took a shaky breath. It was over now; all of it. The knowledge of this sent tears streaking down her cheeks, and she did not wipe them away – she simply let them flow in the same way she let go of the man she loved.

***

I hope you enjoyed this chapter!! Leave your votes and comments on the way out – I'd love to hear what you guys have to say!

# Chapter Twenty-Five

-------------------------------------------------

A/N It's here, it's here! Once again, I'm so sorry for the long wait; but I won't hold you back any longer. Here's this week's update!

IT BEGAN WITH A COUGH. JUST ONE, GENTLE AND UN-THREATENING, AND Lady Victoria Arden assumed that it was a result of nothing more than the cold draft that she had felt brush against her whilst she was walking in the palace grounds outside. It was just a cough, once, and she thought nothing of it.

Now she sat, frailer than she was yesterday, in her bed in the palace; the palace physician stood before her and said, "It is the influenza virus, my lady."

Standing at her bedside, Emmett felt his heart drop into the pit of his stomach. "Will she be all right?" he asked.

"As I am certain you are aware, the virus has known to be life-threatening, Your Lordship," he replied, "but I would remain rather optimistic. After all, Lady Victoria has access to the very best medical services across the land."

"I see. And...and her baby?"

"Your child should be fine, my lord, as long as she receives sufficient care and rest and recovers soon enough."

"So she will get better, won't she?"

"I am unable to promise anything with such certainty, as a man of science I never can; but she has a moderate chance, Sir," the doctor answered carefully, to his dismay. "As I mentioned earlier, influenza has been known to be fatal in some cases, but she is in a good position."

Emmett nodded, swallowing. He had been looking for reassurance from the physician, and he supposed he had gotten some. He looked over at his fiancée beside him. She was dressed in a nightgown, her face pale, her hair more unkempt than either of them were accustomed to. The doctor's words were almost hard to believe, she looked so ill – but she had to get better. She had to – for the child and for herself.

"I will prescribe her some medication, and convey the instructions for its preparation to one of the maids. Make sure she gets plenty of sleep, and does not exert herself." He scribbled something illegible on a slip of paper before starting to pack up his briefcase.

"Yes. Of course. You will see her again?"

"Tomorrow afternoon, Sir."

"Thank you." Emmett nodded. He could not find it in himself to smile.

Neither, it seemed, could the doctor, and his expression remained grave. "No mention, Your Lordship. Take care, my lady."

He left with a curt bow, and Victoria did her best to nod her thanks.

Emmett sat then, in the chair he had placed beside her, and took her hand. "Do not worry yourself, you will recover soon enough."

"I...the baby. If I..." A tear streaked down her cheek, and though she had hardly managed to form a coherent sentence, he understood immediately.

"You will get better, I promise. Do you not remember that the doctor said to remain optimistic?"

"Yes, but..." As if to prove her point, she started to cough. When she had finally recovered, "Please – water."

"Of course." He rushed to attend to her request, and brought a cup of warm water to her lips. She drank gratefully, and when she turned her head away slightly to signal that she had had enough he set the water down on the bedside dresser. "You will be all right, I promise. And the baby will be just fine."

"But the wedding...What if I cannot...recover in time?"

"Then we shall postpone it, my dear, do not let such a detail bother you."

"And you...The virus is...contagious. What if you..."

He shook his head gently, smiling down at her with a gaze more loving than she had ever known. "I will be just fine – I have an excellent immune system. I have seen plenty of disease in my travels, and have never been affected by any of it. Besides, someone shall have to care for you, and if you will be my wife soon enough then I would hope that that someone is me."

She smiled at his words, feeble but no less appreciative. "Thank you. I...I am so lucky...so lucky to be loved by a man like you."

"Well, I am glad that you know it," he jested, chuckling. "Well, Victoria, I advise you rest now. I will send for Prince Javier – I imagine he would be concerned about you...and that seeing him might lift your mood some."

At his words she immediately struggled to sit up, and she winced at the exertion of it. "Wait – Emmett, you...you do not have to—"

He smiled gently, though with an almost unnoticeable hint of sadness in his eyes. "Do not worry yourself over this; I promise I do not mind it at all. You cannot help who you love...and neither can I." He paused. "Speaking of Prince Javier, I will discuss you with him. Perhaps you could still be convinced to marry you – you would be so much happier with him, and I only want what is best for you."

"Emmett, no, I—"

He cleared his throat to clear his mind, standing before she could explain her situation with Javier to him properly. "Victoria, it is fine, really. There is no need to fret over me. I will return as soon as I can. Ring for a maid if you need anything in the meantime."

With that he left the bedroom. She tried to call after him, but her voice caught in her throat, and she slumped back in her pillows, defeated.

Things between Javier and I are over, Emmett, she wanted to tell him. You, on the other hand...you love me so deeply. You would give your life up for me, and I will never be able to thank you enough for it...

And I would never have known that this would happen to me, but perhaps it might be said that I am catching feelings for you too.

***

"EMMELINE!" HE SAW HER IN THE HALLWAY. HE HADN'T MEANT TO FIND her; he was merely looking for Prince Javier, but chanced upon his sister instead.

"What do you want?" she asked glacially.

"Nothing, nothing," he said. "Only to ask if you have seen Prince Javier?"

"And why would you be looking for him?"

"I need to talk to him about Victoria," he answered. "I plan to ask him to marry her."

"Of course this is about her again," she grumbled. "But what makes you think he will say anything different from what he has said all this time?—What makes you think he will have her now?"

"She is sick," he replied. "I do not know if this will work, but I think that perhaps the prospect of losing her forever might awaken something within him."

"Are you not hopelessly in love with her? Why would you try to help her marry him?"

"I am," he answered, "and that is why I must do my best to help her spend the rest of her life with her true love. She does not love me, Emmeline, and I cannot force her to, no matter how much I love her. If she is not happy, I could not be either." He paused. "I know this now, Emmeline. I will not make the mistake I made with you again. I would never forgive myself if I did."

She looked at him for a while, and he wished he could read her thoughts. The ice in her eyes seemed to have melted, but he could not be sure.

Eventually she sighed. "To my knowledge at least, Javier is riding with Alexander. You might catch him by the stables if you are fast enough."

He grinned at her. "Thank you, Linnie."

She nodded in acknowledgement, though she still refused to do so much as crack a smile, before turning and continuing on her way down the hall. Emmett stood where he was and watched her go for a moment, sinking into deep thought. Then he turned and went on his way to the stables.

Meanwhile, however, the princes had already saddled up their horses and started on their way, riding across a field and already a distance away from the stables. Emmett would find the stables empty shortly after, save for the boy cleaning up the recently vacated loose boxes.

"I suppose that what you have to consider, Javier, is whether or not you still love her," Alexander said, as their horses eased into a slow trot. A handful of palace guards lagged a distance behind them for privacy.

"I know your alliance is to your wife these days, Brother, but I pray you remember – she would have married Freddie. Freddie." He sighed. "How can I trust her to love me anymore?"

"Firstly, Javier, you are still my brother," Alexander replied. The two kept moving forward, further and further away from the palace and toward the patch of wood nearby. "Regardless of my relationship with Emmeline – your interests remain one of my greatest priorities." He turned to look at him now. "But this is not about whether she loves you. The question is really whether you love her. If you do, perhaps you should consider giving her a second chance."

"How should I know that she was not only with me for her own gains?—How do I know that she would not have left me the minute Frederick had taken a shine to her, if only he had done so? How could I possibly trust her the way I let myself trust her before?" He shook his head. "I was a fool. High society is full of snakes like her. I should have known better, especially with a set of parents like ours. I of all people ought to be aware that the people we are surrounded by care more for money and power than anything else."

"My question remains the same; do you love her?" Alexander was insistent. "It does not matter if you trust her just yet. Do you love her?"

"She has broken my heart, Alexander, rather irreversibly, and I am quickly losing my affections for her. I do not love her, not as I used to at least, and I shall only care for her less every day."

He looked ahead and quickly changed the subject. "Come, Brother, the wood is in sight now. It's a race!"

And so he sped off, leaving behind a trail of dust and rambunctious laughter; for a brief moment Alexander just watched him go, brow furrowed. Then he pressed his calves against his horse's sides, beginning his chase after his younger brother.

***

WHEN THE ROYAL BROTHERS RETURNED TO THE STABLE THE BOY WHO had helped them ready the horses was still there, and the boxes were clean. Alexander thanked him as he jumped off the horse and the princes handed their steeds over to the boy.

"No mention, Your Highnesses," the young chap answered courteously. He had a muddy face and a lanky frame; he must have not been more than ten. One of the cooks' son, if Alexander remembered correctly; a hardworking lad.

"Oh, yes, do wait a moment, Your Highnesses," he called out, just as the two had passed him by on their way back inside. They turned their heads to look at him and he continued speaking, shouting slightly. "Prince Javier, Earl Portsmouth was lookin' for ya. Said it was urgent – somethin' 'bout a lady, Victoria I think her name was, sick. Very ill, he told me, m'afraid I don't remember what exactly he said about it but it sounded bad to me, Sir."

"Very ill?" he exclaimed; then composed himself quickly. "Thank you, lad. Take this and buy something for yourself when you go shopping for your mother next." He tossed him a coin from his pocket.

"Thank you, Your Highness," the boy cheered, his face lighting up immediately. Javier smiled at him, and though it was barely noticeable, he seemed even more delighted, bowing hurriedly.

The princes left the stables then, and made their way back into the palace. They were silent mostly, except for some light conversation about their horses and the ride they had just enjoyed. Alexander did not pester him about Victoria.

When they arrived at the stairway that would lead to their chambers however, Javier spoke. "I have an errand to run, Brother, I will see you at dinner."

Alexander chuckled. "Off to see her, aren't you?"

"No," he said, all too quickly. "Of course not."

"All right, if you say so." His eyes sparkled mischievously, but he spoke no more of his skepticism. "Till dinner." He ascended the steps and Javier walked toward the guest rooms.

The younger prince would never have expected what he saw. Perhaps if he had, he would not have gone to visit with Victoria to begin with.

***

Hi everyone! It's me :)

Firstly, deepest apologies for the long wait once again. I put this out as soon as I could.

Secondly, I'd just like to say a word about the Wattys. As you may or may not know, neither Artemis nor Apollo got picked for the shortlist; but only about 100 stories were chosen in all of Wattpad, and of those only a couple were historical fiction. The stories that are in there, though, are all really really great, some of them I have read and loved, and I'm really glad they got to be recognised as they deserved to be.

Nonetheless, the Lockhart series remains one of my greatest prides. It's been my first successful dabble in historical fiction and my first project uploaded online, as well as my first series (before this I leaned towards solo novels), and I've found it to have taken courage, perseverance and lots of hard work. I remember the feeling of uploading the blurb of Artemis, and while I was excited and hopeful, I was also terrified. To everyone else who didn't get shortlisted, I hope you keep writing as I will do because the worth of your art is not measured against those of others but rather by the amount of heart you've put into it :)

Okay, cheers everyone, till next time! And a very happy Eid al-Adha to all our Muslim friends :)

Do vote, comment and share! It really does mean a lot to hear back from you guys <3

x Leanne

# Chapter Twenty-Six

UPON HIS RETURN FROM THE STABLES, EMMETT SAT DOWN BESIDE HER again. He watched her rest, completely silent for fear of waking her. Many moments later he could not resist it any longer and reached his hand out to touch her cheek gently. She was beautiful, she would always be beautiful to him, though she did look so sickly, and it broke his heart to see her this way. She stirred, and immediately he retracted his hand from her, a sheepish look overtaking his face. "I'm sorry, I didn't mean to wake you. Pray go back to sleep, you need the rest."

"No, no, there is...there is something I want – need to tell you." She coughed slightly, her throat dry. Without a second thought, Emmett helped to prop her up against some pillows and offered her a glass of water.

"Whatever it is can wait till after you drink this," he said, and she complied. The warm liquid felt thick in her throat, but she drank as much as she could. As she did so he informed her of what had happened.

"I went to look for Prince Javier at the stables – Emmeline told me he would be there with Alexander," he said. "By the time I arrived, however, they had both gone to the wood. I waited for them for some time, but when they did not return after a half hour or so I decided to leave my message with the stable boy and come back to look after you instead."

She held the now-empty cup in her lap. "Princess Emmeline?—Has she forgiven you, finally?"

"I cannot be sure," he replied, "but I do think she is beginning to accept the situation as it is. She pointed me to Prince Javier...but more than that I saw something in her eyes change. She did not look so cold."

"Truly? Oh, that is wonderful." A faint smile surfaced upon her lips.

"Well, it matters not. Soon you will be wed to Prince Javier and her anger is sure to fully subside then anyway."

Her heart sank.

"Then...Then I am sorry," she replied, "for what...for what I am about to say."

He cocked his head ever so slightly, brows furrowing just a fraction, as he waited for her to tell him whatever she had to tell him.

"I...I love you," she blurted out. "I am growing fond of you, more than I would like to admit, and I want to marry you." The exertion of saying the entire sentence in one breath caused her to cough, and Emmett was on his feet instantly, rubbing her back in an attempt to soothe her.

When she was still again, he resumed his seat beside her. "But I thought..."

"Javier...he is selfish. He does not love me. Perhaps he thinks he does...but he takes me for granted," she explained. "He assumes – he does not think of my position. He only thinks of his own. It is...very disappointing." She swallowed. "But you are so kind to me. You love me... You truly do. You do not just claim to. You put me before yourself." She laughed, for the first time in days, weakly but with no less shine in her tired brown eyes. "It is...It is hard not to fall in love with a man like you."

"Are you serious? Oh, do you mean it?" he cried. "Surely you are jesting?"

"Not at all." She smiled at him, a warmth in her eyes directed at him that he had craved for for so long. She meant it – he could feel it in his bones. He remembered something then; something Emmeline had said to him once about her suitor, his best friend. I am unable to explain this, but I can feel it in the marrow of my bones – he will not hurt me. He'd called her silly then, said that one could not feel such a thing. But now he knew exactly what she meant. He knew, because now he too was in love with someone, as he had never been before in all his years.

"But...what about His Highness? I have already sent for him..."

"Do not worry yourself," she said gently, taking his hand. "He will not come."

"And how could you know that...?"

"Because he does not care enough for me to look past his pride," she murmured. "Because he does not love me. He will not see me. We have already said goodbye." She smiled at him again then. "But it does not matter. Now I have you to love...a man who loves me as I would him. More even."

Overjoyed, Emmett seized her hand, and they shared a quiet moment smiling at each other. Neither of the two thought to consider the possibility that Prince Javier had been standing by the doorway ever since Victoria's proclamation of love, and had heard every word.

Now he saw the pair of them, in love like he had once been with her, and felt, acutely, a pang in his heart. Even though he had not intended to take her back, only to see for himself if she would be all right, it hurt him somehow to know that she had moved on from him, from whatever they had shared. He sighed to himself, inaudibly so he wouldn't be caught watching like a fool. He should have known. He had never been destined for love.

***

VICTORIA RECOVERED SOON ENOUGH. IT WAS THE LONGEST FORTNIGHT Emmett had ever experienced, and he was exhausted by the end of it; but seeing her with colour in her cheeks again made being so drained himself completely worth it.

Emmeline had not come to speak to him about anything, and given that he had been completely absorbed in tending to his future wife, he did not go to seek her out either. William had called once, coming by carriage from Wellington House, when the brown-haired young lady was known to be feeling slightly better, and the father and son discussed the situation. Emmett told him about Victoria's newfound feelings for him, and though the duke had never been inclined to show much emotion, the younger Lockhart dared to imagine that he had seen a sparkle in the other man's eye as he had nodded his acknowledgement of her change of heart.

Now he just had to convince his sister that Victoria was not as bad as she might imagine her to be. Emmeline's trust had been betrayed by them both already, her forgiveness crushed when the physician had surprised them all with the news of Victoria's pregnancy. There was no telling if she would be as kind to her prospective sister-in-law as she had previously been.

Either way, he had to try to convince her. So after returning to Wellington House for three full nights of sleep and three full days of rest, Emmett travelled to the castle once more. Victoria had already returned to Westchester for the time being, their wedding arranged to take place in a month and a half (Georgeanne Arden seemed to trust Emmett enough not to rush the ceremony after seeing him care so tirelessly for her daughter). Emmeline's blessings had to be earned by then.

When he knocked gently on the door to her study, the door opened just a crack.

"Who is it, please?" a voice hissed, almost covertly. It was a girl, he could tell that much, but she whispered so quietly he could not distinguish who exactly she was.

In the background he could hear Emmeline laughing, accompanied by a man, also chuckling. He must be interrupting a conversation, he realised, between his sister and Alexander St James. They really did get along rather well, being good friends at least, and it consoled him to know that she had a semblance of bliss.

"Earl Emmett Portsmouth, to see Her Highness, please."

The door opened slightly wider, and a girl slipped out of the study. He knew her clever eyes, and recognised her immediately to be Penelope Smith. She was growing up quickly, her childlike features sharpening as she grew into a young woman, and it warmed his heart a little. Although he had never known her half as well as his sister had, he did see her as a younger relative of sorts, a part of his family – a cousin perhaps; someone he would like to see happy.

"On official business or personal business?"

"Personal business, please, Miss Smith."

She bit her lip, eyes flickering toward the floor as she processed his request. "Can't it wait, Your Lordship?—His Royal Highness and Princess Emmeline are in in the middle of a conversation. Rather important business, I think, not that I was really listening...but Her Highness had me send the other servants out."

She was likely to be the only one trusted enough to be privy to whatever they were saying and allowed to serve them tea while they talked, he surmised.

She turned around briefly, as if to make sure they hadn't noticed that she had left the room. "But more than that I haven't seen her so happy in many days... It took a while for His Highness to coax her into seeing him. He has a way with her..." She shook her head slightly but vigorously, shaking herself out of her absentminded talk. "Not that I have any business speaking to you about this, my lord."

"Is she...Was she upset over me?"

Penelope smiled sadly. "Ever since everything happened with Captain Jamison last year, my lord, there are few moments that she is not."

"It pains me to hear it."

"I'm sure it does," she murmured regretfully. Then, clearing her throat, "Would you care to wait in one of the drawing rooms? I will inform Princess Emmeline that you came to call once she finishes speaking with Prince Alexander."

"I would appreciate that," he said, also forcing himself to lift his own mood. "Thank you."

"Not at all, Sir," she said. "Where would you like to wait? Most of them are empty at the moment, I think."

"I'll just be in the nearest one down the hall."

"Would you like me to send for tea for you? Or something to eat?"

"No, thank you, Miss Smith – Lady Penelope. I shall be quite content waiting."

"Very well, my lord," she said, bobbing a quick curtsy. "If you would excuse me then...I must return to refill their tea."

Then she disappeared back into the study, and he turned to walk down the hall to the drawing room. There he waited, patient, wondering about what the two were talking about five doors away.

After what felt to him like a good half of an hour the door opened, and he stood eagerly to greet his sister. He caught a glimpse of her husband disappearing down the hallway – presumably he had walked her here – before she nodded in greeting.

"Good evening, Emmett," she said. "Penny said you wanted to speak with me."

"Yes," he said. "Victoria and I are getting married in about five weeks...out of love, I promise, she loves me now as I love her. It would mean the world to me if I might have your blessing."

She raised one eyebrow, folding her arms across her chest. "And why would you ever need such a thing?—You have seemed perfectly content with acting before discussing anything with me first for a long time now."

He sighed. "You know this. You are my sister, Linnie, the most important woman in the world to me. I could never get married in peace knowing that you disapprove."

"Really? How curious – for many months now you've seemed to want to get married against my will, so it does come as a surprise that now you would feel uncomfortable marrying anyone without my approval," she scoffed. "Besides, whatever happened to never marrying anyone you love, for naught but the sake of tormenting yourself – whatever happened to that noble cause?"

"Emmeline...things changed," he said. "I stopped my self-sabotaging behaviour because of you. Have you forgotten what we said in the rose garden already? You showed me that I have been f—"

"I don't want you to marry her," she said sharply, interrupting him.

"P-Pardon?" he sputtered, eyes wide.

"You said that you could not marry anyone in peace knowing that I disapprove," she clarified. "I do not want you to marry Victoria Arden. Call the wedding off."

"Emmeline..."

"Either that, or prove to me that she loves you. Have her come to the castle at once." Her tone was icy and firm. He knew at once that there would be no changing her mind.

"But she is already in Westchester, she must only have arrived two days ago—"

"If she loves you then she will travel back to London," she retorted instantly. "Or are you afraid that she does not love you as you love her?"

"No," Emmett replied, sighing. "Very well...I shall send her a letter immediately."

***

Thank you guys so much for reading, voting, and commenting! (Please vote and comment! I really love to hear from you guys and it really makes my day getting a comment from any of you!)

Fun fact about me – I'm currently listening to Russell Dickerson's Yours EP on loop. It's so feel-good and fun and I really like music like that. I also love country music, although I'm not sure I'd safely classify Russell Dickerson under country music. Country-pop perhaps?

# Chapter Twenty-Seven

A/N Hi everyone! Sorry that this is a couple days late :d I'm in the middle of exams (again! when does it ever end?)...I'll do my best to be as punctual as possible though. Not that there's much of Apollo left to go – it draws to a close on Chapter Thirty!

ALEXANDER PRESSED A KISS TO HER FOREHEAD BEFORE HE LEFT HER study. "I'm glad you're feeling better," he said, squeezing her hand, and then he slipped out the door. He passed his brother-in-law and his fiancée on the way out, and offered them a nod, that said both good morning and good luck.

Emmett knocked, and Penelope Smith opened the door with a slight smile. "Good morning, Your Lordship. Good morning, Lady Victoria," she greeted. "Her Highness has been expecting you."

"Thank you, Lady Penelope," Emmett answered; and a lady she was, for as they entered the room she curtsied with not half the clumsiness she used to have about her, her easy manner in fact slightly reminiscent of Emmeline in her own younger days.

"Well, good morning to both of you," the princess was seated at her desk when she entered, not smiling, but her eyes betrayed no anger. She seemed to be in pleasant enough spirits, and this lifted her brother's hopes enough.

"I must say, Lady Victoria, I am surprised," she continued. "I did not think you loved my brother enough to come all the way here at such short notice."

"Your Highness, I—"

"Or perhaps you only travelled for the baby? So that it might have a father and you would not be so disgraced, since you have been shunned by Prince Javier?"

"Princess, please, I love Earl Portsmouth. I love Emmett," Victoria said. Emmeline saw a certain genuineness in her brown eyes, but still this girl had to be put to the test.

So she replied, "Words mean nothing."

"But—"

"That is why I called you here to prove it to me," she told her. "You should be aware, however, of this one condition: if you, in any way, demonstrate that you are lying to me, I will ruin you. You should know that I would do anything for my brother's sake." She paused momentarily, allowing her words to sink in. "Do you still wish to marry him? Say you do not and you shall be allowed to return home. And—I will be able to broker you a marriage with Prince Javier."

"H-How?" she asked. "He has been very clear..."

Emmett felt his heart rise to his throat at the sight of her wavering, but said nothing. This was a test, he knew it, and she had to pass it on her own merit.

"Alexander spoke with him," the princess replied coolly. "He is not steadfast in his position. He can and will be easily swayed...should you only give the word."

Victoria paused, and Emmett could feel his heart ricocheting in his chest.

Then, she said, "No."

"No?" Emmeline repeated, sounding somewhat pleasantly surprised but not betraying much else as her expression remained neutral.

"My heart belongs to Earl Portsmouth now. Even if Javier should still be interested in having a relationship with me...I am not interested in having one with him." She sighed. "I was considering it for my baby...I would have wanted him to know his father. But Emmett is his father now, and that is all that needs to be known to him."

"Understood, thank you." Emmeline nodded before looking down at a sheet of paper in front of her, and her brother could have sworn that he had caught a glimpse of some approval in her green eyes.

"Well, then, I will not exert you terribly since you are with child," she went on. "You may retire to of it the guest rooms to rest – I have ordered servants to ready them for you. I shall see you at luncheon."

Victoria rose and bobbed a curtsy, before a smiling maid came to see her to her room. She left the room then, leaving the siblings alone.

Emmeline turned to her brother then, eyebrows slightly raised. "Emmett, would you care for a turn about the orchard? I would like to speak to you about the... situation."

"The weather today is rather lovely – the orchard sounds pleasant enough."

"Wonderful," Emmeline murmured, standing. Together they walked into the hallway, followed by Penelope Smith, who dutifully held the door open for them.

Turning to her lady-in-waiting, the princess then said, "Penny, will you tell the cooks that Emmett, Lady Victoria and I will be dining in the dining room in about two hours?—And do prepare some tea and desserts for us as well. Martha's latest macaron recipe has been rather well-loved, I think Emmett and Lady Victoria would also enjoy those."

"Of course, my lady. I shall notify the chefs and begin brewing the tea immediately." The girl curtsied deeply before hurrying down the hall.

Emmett was smiling in amusement as he looked upon his sister. "Why, does the lass still call you 'my lady'?"

"Yes, well, 'Your Highness' sounds terribly cold," she answered. "To be quite honest I would have her call me by my first name, and I have requested it a number of times, but she has always refused. Perhaps in a few years – I don't know."

"The pair of you have always been close."

"Like sisters," Emmeline agreed. "She has always been there for me...ever since Mother passed and..."

"Indeed." He sighed. "I am grateful to her. For through everything I put you through – she was there with you, when I was too selfish to be."

"She is very sweet girl," she said. Then, changing the subject, "Would you care to explain your affections for Lady Victoria Arden? I have given it all ample thought...I must not know her as you do. If you sound reasonable enough, perhaps I might be better convinced to approve of your marriage."

"Of course," he replied, looking out into the orchard below them as they neared it, walking through a hall on a higher storey. "Well, first it was her keen mind that drew me to her; she has a true love for knowledge, she craves it as you do, and that I something I respect greatly. Perhaps...It is possible, on hindsight, that it was first endearing to me because it reminded me of you."

"Being clever can also mean being conniving," she answered, "and we are both aware of how she has connived to worm her way into power through marriage."

"Actually, speaking of that," he said, a light smile touching his face. "I have come to see for myself that she is good at heart. All of her 'conniving', as you call it...all of it she was forced to do. She told me of it – you see, I had a number of opportunities to speak with her during our residency at the university..."

And he told her everything, all the times they had met in hallways, in courtyards, in libraries, and of everything she had told him. How the duchess had threatened to burn her books, but how despite all that her mother had said to her she still believed that the old shrew only wanted the best for her...

Emmeline listened as he talked, on and on and on, but the content of his words did not matter so much as the light in his eyes. She saw it now – he was in love with the girl, truly, madly and deeply. Emmeline had suspected his affections for duke's daughter to be deep and genuine when he tended to her throughout her illness, but now she knew it to be a fact. For she too would have had such a light in her eyes if she were to speak of her true love...but his name no longer had any business on her tongue. He was a part of her past, and with what the King had decreed, banishing him from her presence for the rest of his career, he would never be a part of her future.

And as if summoned by her thoughts, she saw her future walking toward them as they returned indoors for luncheon.

"Emmeline, beloved," he greeted, grinning. Then, with a respectful nod, "Portsmouth."

"Good afternoon, Alexander," she answered, smiling. "My brother and I were just on a walk around the orchard. It really is a beautiful day today."

"It is indeed." He smiled gently at his wife. Perking up slightly, he turned to his brother-in-law. "Well, then, how was your walk?"

All three of them knew that he was not referring to the weather.

"Quite delightful," Emmett replied. "You have a beautiful orchard."

"It is all my mother's doing," the prince replied, sounding pleased at the answer he had received. "But I am glad to hear that you enjoyed yourselves."

"We must be on our way to luncheon now," Emmeline cut in. "I invited Lady Victoria to dine with us today, and it would not do to keep her waiting."

"Of course," Alexander responded. "I will see you at dinner then, my dear?"

"You will." She smiled at him. "Till dinner."

And so they each went on their way, the twins to the dining room and the prince to his private library.

***

LADY VICTORIA, IN THE MEANTIME, WAS ROUSED FROM HER NAP BY A maid, and helped into her dress. The maid then led her to the dining room, where Emmett and Emmeline were already waiting at their seats, with the princess at the head of the table and looking as intimidating as she always did.

"I hope you rested well, Lady Victoria?" Emmeline asked in greeting, and she sounded pleasant enough, although her countenance showed no amicability.

"Yes, Your Highness – wonderfully, in fact. Thank you for your hospitality," Victoria replied smilingly, as she knew she was expected to, and offered the princess a curtsy. Then, turning to the man in the room, she curtsied again. "Good afternoon, Your Lordship."

She might call him Emmett privately, for their relationship warranted a certain degree of intimacy; but in the presence of others they were only engaged and had no business being so casual with one another.

"Have a seat, then, I am ravenous already," Emmeline said.

She complied, and the appetisers were served.

"So," the princess began. "Tell me about yourself."

"My name is Victoria Catherine Arden, Your Highness, and I am twenty and three," she said. "I grew up in Westchester with my dear father, my mother, and my sisters. I am the oldest child in my family."

Taking a bite of her greens, Emmeline nodded, signalling for her to keep talking.

"My father believes, strongly, in educating women. He employed a tutor for my sisters and myself the moment I learned to speak. Since then I have fallen deeply in love with academia of all kinds – I am, however, partial to science over the humanities."

"I see." She paused thoughtfully. "Would you call yourself a selfish person?"

"Well, I...perhaps. Yes." She took a sip of the glass of water beside her dish, and she clutched the glass so tightly Emmeline could see her knuckles turn white.

Still the princess was unrelenting. "Would you care to expound on that?"

"I...Well, I cannot recall doing a single selfless thing in my life," she replied. "I...Unfortunately, I have never been a situation that called for me to make sacrifices for others. I suppose...I suppose it might be said, to put it bluntly, that I am rather spoiled."

"Do you love your father?"

"Yes." This time the girl did not have to hesitate for a second, and she was grateful for such an easy question.

"Would you give your life for him?"

"Yes. If it would save him from suffering I would die a million deaths for him."

"And do you not think your child has caused him suffering?" Emmeline went on to ask. "Do you not think you have caused him pain with your carelessness?"

"I am certain that I have," she said, casting her eyes to the table briefly before meeting the other girl's gaze once more. "But there is little more I can do to make it up to him now. The best I can do is to settle myself in a stable and happy marriage...I am sure his worries will be greatly eased if I am married to a man I love deeply, and can bear this child to a complete family with two parents present."

"I see." Emmeline nodded. "Is the salad to your liking?"

"Yes – the greens are very fresh. And the dressing is absolutely delicious."

"Well, the chefs will be pleased to hear it." She took time to chew on another bite of her salad, and there was a brief silence. Victoria took another drink of water, emptying her glass once again, and a maid hurried forth to refill it.

"You have mentioned a lot about your father – tell me about your mother," Emmeline said, her tone misleadingly light, as if she did not know what kind of answer the seemingly harmless question would warrant in Victoria Arden's case.

"My mother...well," she tried to answer, but a description of the duchess did not come easily to her. "She is very...She tries to—She is...good at securing the best interests for her family."

"I can see that," the princess answered coolly. "Is it true that she tried to force you to catch Frederick as your husband, even when you were in a relationship with Javier?"

"Y—Yes. She talked of my duties to my father, and she threatened to burn my books...but forgive me, Your Highness, let us please discuss something else. I cannot speak ill of her, I cannot. She is my mother."

"And do you love her, as you love your father?"

"I love her, I do, though perhaps not as I love my father – we have different relationships, you might say, in that she tries to make me a better lady whereas my father tries to help me become a better person."

"That is an interesting way to put it." She took a sip of her tea. "Well, then, do you love my brother?—I have asked you this question before."

"You have, Madam, and my answer is different this time. I do, I love Emmett, with all of my heart."

"And you would like to be married to him why?"

"So that I might better love him, for the rest of our lives."

Emmeline cracked a smile at that answer. The rest of the table conversation was far easier for Victoria Arden to endure, and through the main course and over dessert they discussed her upbringing, her aspirations, and what she might hope to name her child.

***

# Chapter Twenty-Eight

A/N Hoorah for punctual updates! Here's this week's chapter – prepare for what ought to be the last bit of drama for Apollo!!

"SHE DID NOT DISAPPOINT AT ALL, DID SHE?" EMMETT RE-MARKED WITH A wide grin once his fiancée had left the dining room at the end of their meal so that the siblings could speak privately.

"I still worry," his sister confessed. "I would trust no one with your heart, you know it. But I have no choice but to believe what she says...believe that this is not merely an act. I have to because you love her, and I could never bear to keep you from the woman you love."

"So we have your blessing?"

"Yes." She smiled, resigned. "Emmy—I want you to know that if she really ever does swindle you of your fortune – but heaven forbid she does, for I will destroy her if she has the gall to even entertain such a notion –, you will never be turned away from my door."

"She will do no such thing. I know it, you need not fret over it." He chuckled. "Though I must admit that living in St James' Palace does not sound like a bad contingency plan. It is the most lavish home I have ever visited."

"I would imagine that that is to be expected," she replied dryly with an amused smile. Then, she asked keenly, "When exactly is the wedding? Do you need any help?"

"All I need from you now is your presence."

"You shall have it," she answered, a shadow of her smile still lingering on her lips. "I am happy for you, Emmett. I am happy that you are happy."

He hesitated. "What about you and the good prince?"

"Well, I would not have chosen this for myself, perhaps, but I am happy being married to him. He is good to me, and I try not to think of the other things that could have been – that has never brought anyone any joy," she said. "He is one of my greatest comforts...and my dearest friend."

"I thought I was your dearest friend," he exclaimed jestingly.

She laughed, and it was no less than music to his ears. "Not with all the headaches you have caused me recently over this Victoria Arden business, I'm afraid you are not."

"I'm sorry," he said, "I really am. For everything that has happened. But we will both be married very soon, and hopefully we can be once again the siblings we once were."

"We have always been the siblings we once were, Emmett, for what else has our conflict been borne of but love?" She smiled. "But I do know what you mean to say. Yes—hopefully we shall have less to fight over."

They were silent for a while, both thinking of all that had happened in the past year or so. They had both changed, as had their entire situation. Peter had gone away, to patrol the colonies, and Emmeline was a princess now. Victoria Arden was no longer considered an obnoxious threat, and Emmett was engaged to her and about to be a father. Perhaps neither of their situations were ideal – for she might have preferred being a captain's wife, and he might have wanted to be the father of his own child instead of Prince Javier's – but they were both happy, and they were together, and that was enough.

***

DESPITE WHAT EMMETT HAD SAID ABOUT NOT NEEDING HER HELP, Emmeline decided that she would most definitely have a hand in her brother's wedding. She offered them the palace chapel and engaged a bishop to officiate the ceremony. The royal seamstresses would tailor all their clothes, and the chefs were going into town to buy produce, as well as amending and upscaling their recipes as they prepared to cook up a storm.

Before that, however, she had also announced that there would be an engagement party. Presently they were all getting ready to attend it, Emmett, Victoria, Duke Mayfair, and the Arden family all placed in guest rooms; the royal family in their own quarters.

Not bothered by the fact that palace servants were present in the room helping them powder their faces, Georgeanne Arden decided that it would be wise to speak badly of the princess – as she so loved to do, for in her eyes Emmeline Lockhart was a snake who had stolen her precious firstborn's future husband.

"Isn't that Lockhart girl so vicious!" she exclaimed. "And pretentious! Look at her, throwing you this party as if she is not out to get you, my darling?"

Victoria said nothing.

"First she has stolen your rightful husband, and now she will take away your baby's father – I know it, I know it already! This is all an act, and sooner or later she will make sure Emmett Lockhart never marries you. Just you wait and see."

Still her daughter remained silent, unwilling to engage with such talk.

"She has her claws in every man she knows, I will tell you that much. She won't let anyone have them – the last time I met her, that snake—"

"Enough!" Finally she could take it no longer. "Forgive me Mother, for being so direct about what I am about to say, but you are about ten times more vicious than Her Highness will ever be! And I say 'Her Highness', Mother, not 'that snake', because that is how she deserves to be addressed, even when she is not in the room. She is royalty, she is our princess, and she will one day be our Queen. You would do well to remember it!"

Turning to the maids in the room, she lowered her voice to a normal volume and said, trembling, "Please leave us for a minute."

They did not need to be told twice, and streamed out of a service door, tittering nervously.

Watching as her daughter raised her voice against her for what must have been the first time in her life, Georgeanne's expression shifted, her eyes narrowing. "Why, how dare you turn on me for a wretch like her—"

"She is no wretch, Mother, and she is not a snake. She has only shown love and kindness – to her brother, and to me! She has shown me forgiveness you never would have!"

"What is there to forgive you for, Victoria, you have done nothing wrong!"

"I have eroded her trust in her brother, that is what I have done," she said, "and now I am marrying him to bear him a child that he never fathered!"

There was an ear-shattering silence in the room as the weight of her confession settled on all their shoulders – Georgeanne's, Victoria's, and all her sisters'.

"What...What is that supposed to mean?" the duchess asked, pale as a sheet.

"My child...It is not Earl Portsmouth's."

"Then...whose...?"

Victoria closed her eyes and exhaled shakily. This had been a secret that she'd intended to keep, from her mother more than anyone else in the world. "That is a detail you need not know."

"I can hardly believe it." Georgeanne scoffed. "My oldest daughter, my greatest pride, is no better than a common whore."

"Mama, don't say that," one of Victoria's younger sisters squeaked, sounding rather terrified.

"Shut your mouth, you are not a part of this conversation!"

She was silenced immediately.

Georgeanne was silent for a while before she spoke again. "Emmeline Lockhart knows about this?"

"Yes. And she forgave me for it." Victoria thrust her chin up slightly, as if to stand up to her mother still, trying to convince herself that she was strong enough to withstand anything the duchess might throw her way.

"Does she know who the father is?"

"Yes."

"So you would tell her, but not me...How laughable." She shook her head. "Victoria...I will never admit to having a daughter like you. You have humiliated me, through and through – that you might trust in a stranger more than your own mother. That you might have lied to me all this time...that you have been giving yourself away, probably to some peasant you are so ashamed of behind my back. You dishonour me."

The girl told herself that she was strong, but still tears ran down her cheeks. "I...I'm sorry, Mother. I never meant for it to be this way."

"Come now, girls. We will not attend this celebration...there is nothing to be celebrated. The whole situation is absolutely disgusting." And she picked herself up from her chair and left the room. Her daughters followed meekly, none daring to protest, or even to offer a sympathetic word to their older sister.

Once the room had been emptied, Victoria took a deep breath. She won't make me cry...I should have known. Mother...She would never have forgiven me, she does not love me more than she loves the reputation I could bring her. I should have stood up to her years ago. This falling out – it is for the better...

And she wept.

***

"WHERE IS VICTORIA?" EMMETT ASKED, NOTICING THAT HIS BRIDE-TO-BE was conspicuously missing from her own engagement party. "Actually, where is her entire family?"

He craned his neck to look over all the moving heads in the room, hoping to catch a glimpse of any of the Ardens. "None of them are here. It is unlike any of them to be late to a party, even fashionably so."

"Would you like me to send someone to look for them?" Emmeline asked.

"That would be marvellous, Linnie, thank you."

She beckoned to a maid standing in a corner, looking for someone to serve a drink to. The servant hurried over, and Emmeline whispered a few words in her ear. With a nod, she left the room in search of the missing few.

It took a few moments for her to return.

"Your Highness," she said to Emmeline, "His Grace and Lady Victoria have requested Earl Portsmouth's audience, as well as your own. They are in the room we have allocated her – something appears to be wrong."

And so the siblings hurried to them, neither speaking a word the whole way there, each of them silently wondering what on earth could have happened to cause such a disruption.

Victoria was sitting on the ottoman in front of the bed and sobbing when they entered the room, the agony in her cries catching Emmett completely off-guard. He went to her immediately, and took her in his arms, whispering consolations and sweet nothings in her ear, hoping that he could make it stop. Her father stood in the corner of the room, looking rather upset himself, his brow furrowed, his jaw set.

"What has happened here?" Emmeline asked. "It is a merry occasion."

The duke sighed. "Victoria's mother...she found out about the child."

"Pray, Westchester, what about the child did the duchess find out?"

"It is not your brother's, Your Highness...but you already knew it." There was pain in his eyes as he said it. "I do not blame you. I only wish my daughter would have been honest with me. I hardly have anything to say to her...I am sorely disappointed in her. As her mother is."

"Lady Victoria was in a difficult position," Emmeline replied, surprising everyone in the room as she stood up for the girl whom she previously would have sought to get rid of at any given opportunity. "I hope you empathise with her, Duke Westchester, she needs your support now more than ever."

"Of course, Madam," he said. "And I do. But I did not raise her to—"

"The baby, do you know whose it is?" Emmeline interrupted once his rising volume began to betray his anger. "Do you know the exact circumstances under which your daughter lied to you?"

He spoke quietly again. "...No. I do not."

"Then allow me to tell you that Victoria was shirked in the most cruel of ways," Emmeline said. "Only when she was pregnant did the father decide he did not wish to commit to her. He told her to have the child and raise it alone – that all he could give her was a doctor and money. She tried to win him back, and I did as well on her behalf, but he would not relent. He would not listen to her, and she could hardly do a thing about it – for the child's father is my brother-in-law Prince Javier. What would you have liked her to say against a prince? How could her word possibly mean more than his, in the world we live in?"

"I..." His eyes showed how torn he was. Part of him wanted to hold his daughter in a tight embrace, to vow that he would always be on her side, but the other half of his heart blamed her for not telling him about any of this from the start, for hiding things from him.

"My brother decided to take responsibility. While I did not approve of it then, and perhaps I would still choose to stop him if I had been given the chance to – how could anyone blame your daughter for accepting help in such a dire situation?"

David was silent for a long while. "I just wish you would have told me sooner, Victoria. I would have believed you, you know I would have."

The girl pulled away from Emmett to answer him. "I know, Papa, I know, and I'm so sorry. I was just...I was so scared...I didn't know what would happen...I didn't want Mother to find out...I knew she would disown me...! And now she has, and I..."

"Come here, my dear." He opened his arms to her, and immediately she leapt into them, and began weeping anew. "It's all right – I understand now. Everything will be just fine."

***

I can hardly believe that the Lockhart series is coming to an end (it's really just Artemis, Apollo and Yuletide with Will)...it's been my baby for the past one-and-a-half/two years and I really just can't bear to see it go :( I don't think there'll be any further sequels after this. I feel like by Chapter 30 the story will be right where it ought to be, and everything will have been wrapped up really nicely.

Just a quick confession; I feel a little lost about what I'll work on next. I was thinking of dabbling in fantasy (which I've never done before ever, so it does sound super cool!) but I really don't know. Let me know if you have any ideas/preferences on where my creative direction should go next!

x Leanne

# Chapter Twenty-Nine

LadyRowynundefined for being here since my earliest days writing on Wattpad and always being so supportive!! This one's for you! Thank you so much You've been something of a mentor for me and after every update I find myself waiting on your comment. You've been asking for this forever, and since the series is coming to an end, I thought I'd just do it. Enjoy!

THE FOUR OF THEM ENTERED THE BALLROOM TOGETHER ONCE VICTORIA had had her makeup redone and her red eyes soothed as far as they could be. The rest of the night was uneventful, and everyone was glad for it. There was music and dancing and laughter and plenty of delectable hors d'oeuvres, the guests fawned over the engaged couple, and Emmett and Victoria were more in love than ever.

At the end of the day, the guests left the castle slightly intoxicated and giggling, and the Lockharts and Ardens and St Jameses who had attended the party returned to their rooms for some much-needed rest. That is, all but Emmeline and Alexander, who retreated to the prince's private library for a late-night conversation.

"That was a splendid party, beloved, congratulations," he said as he pulled out a chair for himself.

She laughed, settling into a snug sofa beside him and pulling her feet up to tuck them under her legs. "Why, thank you. It might have been better if you hadn't hoarded all of my dances, there were plenty of guests I should have been talking to."

"Well, in that case I'm terribly sorry," he answered, equally teasing, "but I could hardly help myself. You are simply enchanting."

She laughed again, but she also started to blush then, her cheeks turning cherry red. As she gazed upon him, in the dim candlelight that they used to light the otherwise dark room, she noticed for perhaps the first time just how handsome he was, not just in terms of his sharp jaw and defined cheekbones but also in terms of the slight sparkle in his eye and the way he smiled at her. In that moment, she suddenly found herself feeling a feeling she hadn't felt for months now – since she'd last seen Peter. Her heart skipped a beat as she realised this.

They were only supposed to be friends – married but not in love. That had been the arrangement, and anything else felt strange.

And her heart...was it still owned by another?—She tried to think of Captain Peter Jamison and look away, but all she could see was her husband in front of her, and her eyes remained fixed on him. She realised that, with all the recent dramatics in her life, she had not thought of her former flame in a long time...and that in her darkest days of late she had found solace in this man in front of her. He made her laugh, he held her when she cried, and if there was anything she wanted he would go to the moon and back if it meant that she would have it. She did not know if Peter would ever have done the same for her – after all, he was never given the chance to love her as his wife, and he had chosen his career over her.

And she had never been allowed the opportunity to love Peter as she now loved this man. Peter was her suitor, but he had never been family. Her brown-haired, hazel-eyed captain had made her feel like a princess... Being married to Alexander had actually made her princess, but more than that the light-haired, blue-eyed Prince Charming before her made her feel like a queen. Was it betrayal to ever let herself love another man when she had promised her heart to Peter already...? Would it be fair to herself to never open her heart to anyone in her life, especially if she already knew that she would likely never again see Peter in her lifetime?—Should her past mean that she should never have romance in her future? Should Peter even be considered part of her past, when he was still out there, somewhere far away, perhaps still thinking of her?

Meanwhile he looked into her eyes, so green, shining in the candlelight, with her rosy cheeks illuminated by a yellow flame. She was aglow, reminiscent of an angel, and to him she was such an angel...such a blessing, with such a keen sense of humour and such a genuine heart and such a brilliant mind, with such great passion and such strong determination. He felt his breathing grow shallower and his heartbeat quicken just at the sight of her.

He loved her – in more ways than one, he now understood. He had always known that he loved her as a family member, as his dearest friend, as the one person in the universe who would always be by his side...but could he ever love her as anything else? Would she ever want him to? Did he already?

Perhaps it was the flutes of champagne that the both of them had downed during the party that blurred their judgement slightly, or perhaps it was the heat of the moment. Either way, neither of them found themselves wanting to give any of it too much thought – more than anything, they both wanted to live in the moment, and think of the consequences, moral or emotional, after.

"Can I...can I kiss you?" he asked, his voice barely a whisper.

And she found herself nodding 'yes'.

***

THE DAY OF THE WEDDING WAS DRAWING NEARER. AND WHAT A marvellously grand affair it would be – for huge efforts had gone into preparations for it from all parties. Both Emmett and Victoria were deeply invested in planning for the ceremony. Emmeline insisted on helping the couple get the very best of everything – food, decorations, invitations, flowers, clothes... Bethany Rutherford was responsible for overseeing the decoration of the palace chapel, and she beamed with pride all the while. Both her niece and nephew had found respectable partners, and the grandeur of it all made her giddy. And she would be attending the wedding in her sister Anne's place!—The very thought of it made her want to dance.

The fathers William and David were temporarily living in the castle, along with Emmett and Victoria, for convenience's sake. They wished to assist others in the preparations, but usually found themselves at a loss about how they could be of any help or hindering operations instead, and mostly spent their time reading, discussing matters of the court, or on long walks around the palace grounds.

And everyone was, of course, having new clothes of the finest quality fitted for them, on Emmeline's decree. Victoria's wedding dress would be the most costly of all, and Emmett was determined to pay for it himself. Emmeline let him.

When the day of the ceremony finally fell upon them, the palace chapel was packed with guests. Victoria Arden found herself standing where Emmeline had not so long ago, her father by her side, preparing to change her name.

"I will miss you, my dear," he said, patting her hand. "The house will be so empty without you."

"Oh, Papa..." Her eyes prickled with tears. "How will you deal with Mother on your own?"

"I will manage, Victoria, I have for decades now." He chuckled. "I will admit, however, that life will certainly be less bearable without you. Who else will I take to the library every evening?"

"Delilah mentioned...she told me once that she wanted to come with us. You ought to take her, Papa, if you can." A tear slipped down her cheek, and though his own eyes were red, David looked alarmed.

"Now, now, don't cry, darling, you look beautiful and your makeup will be ruined." Fishing a handkerchief out from his pocket, he daubed gently at her eyes. "Don't cry. This is a wonderful occasion."

"I—I cannot imagine living away from you," she choked out. "You will be all the way in Westchester! And I will be in Portsmouth."

"Portsmouth is beautiful, my dear, have you not always loved the sea?"

"I know, and I have, but – but it is so far from you..."

"I promise to visit often," he said. "You are always welcome home as well."

"I know, I know, but..."

"Emmett Lockhart loves you dearly," he said, "and you love him also. You will be happy there, I promise. Marriages of love are a blessing unlike any other, Victoria, a blessing I never received. I hope you treasure it."

"I wish I could be with him without marrying!" she cried, and it was likely the most improper thing she had said all her life, with perhaps the exception of when she had rebuked her mother before her engagement party.

"Everyone must marry," he replied gently. "You are no exception, Victoria, it would pain me to see you a spinster. For if you never marry, who will take care of you when you are old and I have gone?"

"I know, I know all this." She sniffled. "I just wish..."

"Whatever you wish, my dear, I assure you I wish it even more. But let us not speak of it, it will only make this harder. And today should not be a day for grief."

"Oh, Papa, I love you."

"As I love you, my darling."

"I—" She was about to say something else when the doors to the nave opened, and she had to tighten her grip around her father's arm and walk through them.

She knew that her life would never be the same.

***

AND IT WAS NEVER THE SAME AGAIN. WHEN SHE ENTERED THE ROYAL ballroom for the party following her wedding ceremony that evening she was on her new husband's arm, not her father's, and she would likely never be presented to a crowd on her father's arm again. The crier announced their presence, addressing them as Earl Emmett Portsmouth and Lady Victoria Lockhart. All eyes turned to look upon the newlyweds, and instantly there was audible gushing about how lovely they looked together. When they went to greet the princess and their fathers, who were standing together in a nearby corner of the ballroom, Emmeline laughed at this, and was just about to tease her brother about it when her own husband appeared before her and whisked her away for a dance.

"Is Javier in attendance?" she asked him as they waltzed slowly.

"I don't believe so," he answered with a slight frown. "He feigned disinterest, but I reckon that he feels rather shunned. He is probably off drinking, as he tends to do whenever anything upsets him."

"Well, he had his chance with her," she sighed, "and unfortunately he chose to let her go – even when Lady Victoria was nearly on her knees begging."

There was some regret in his eyes as he nodded in agreement. "Indeed he did."

They would later find Javier missing, his horse gone from the stable, with nothing but a letter left behind. It would say that he was unhappy in the castle, in court, and that the wedding of the woman he still had some feelings for to another man had been the last straw for him. It would say not to look for him, that he would return home when he was ready to; that he was off to find himself again, to live a life that he loved. As Prince Alexander read the letter aloud, everyone in the room knew instantly that it meant that he was likely headed toward academic study; but no one said anything, for no one intended to go after him. He needed time to find peace and perhaps even happiness, and they all knew it.

But in that moment none of it mattered, because none of it was known unto them yet. Princess Emmeline looked over at her brother and his fiancée, both of whom looked absolutely enamoured with one another. She smiled lightly – her brother looked so happy. Then she looked into her husband's eyes and felt his arms around her, so reassuring, so full of love. Things were finally settling down, and she was glad for it. She'd had enough melodrama in the past year or so to last her a lifetime.

***

Hey everyone! I'm a little emotional right now because this is the second last update on Apollo. I would start talking about how grateful I am for all the love this story has received – and I am super grateful! – but that, I think, is better saved for the Afterword. So, as always, vote, comment, and share this story...and for the last time, till next Friday! *escapes to a corner to cry*

# Chapter Thirty - PART ONE

----------------------------------------

All right, so there's been a bit of a complication...I had most of Chapter Thirty ready but then I found it too rambly and I didn't want to end Apollo off with a chapter that didn't really have much value. So I've begun rewriting, but the full chapter isn't ready yet. As such the last chapter of Apollo will be uploaded in parts – and here's the first. Enjoy!

THE TEMPEST OUTSIDE ROARED AS IT DROVE A RAGGED BLADE OF LIGHT into the Earth, and as if in synchronisation with the deafening thunder, Princess Emmeline screamed. Her husband and brother heard this from where they sat in the next room, Emmett holding his young son on his lap. Despite all the ruckus, the toddling young nobleman was fast asleep, his face buried in his father's chest. The three-year-old David Lockhart had, thankfully, inherited all of Victoria's features, and his chocolate brown eyes and curly chocolate locks rendered him a most adorable young lad.

"It sounds terrible over there," Prince Alexander said worriedly, casting a glance at the door as if he hoped to see his wife walk through it with a baby in her arms any minute now. "I'm not sure I want more children after this. I couldn't make her endure such agony a second time."

"It broke my heart to see Victoria go through such pain as well, but David was the best thing to ever happen to us. She thinks him worth all her suffering, and I am certain that your child will bring just as much light to Emmeline's life as this one has to mine. Victoria is already asking for more children, you know." He smiled. "Do not worry yourself. Both my Aunt Beth and Victoria are by her side, and both of them have had children of their own before – I promise they will make sure that Emmeline is all right."

"I suppose," he replied, sighing. "I wish I could bear her pain for her."

Emmett chuckled. "Do not underestimate my sister, Alexander. She might just have a higher tolerance for pain than you do."

"Again, perhaps you are right." The crown prince sighed again.

The thunder rumbled outside. There was a pause before Emmeline screamed again, the loudest yet this time, and Victoria could be heard speaking to her, urgently and encouragingly, though her exact words were muffled by the wall between them. Emmeline screamed again, and then there was silence for a brief moment.

Then the cries of a baby could be heard.

"She's done it!" Emmett cried, sounding just as triumphant as his sister must have looked in the next room. He shook his son gently. "David, David, lad, wake up now. Your Aunt Emmeline's had her baby, we'll be called in any minute to see her."

"Baby?" David murmured, rubbing the sleep from his eyes with his little fists. "Aunt Linnie's baby?"

"Yes, Aunt Linnie's baby. Would you like to meet it?"

"Yes," the toddler answered with a few nods, barely coherent. "B-Baby."

He chuckled, setting David on his feet. "All right. Wake up, then."

Alexander smiled at his wobbling nephew and tried imagining having a little human of his own to love as Emmett loved David. Would the child be a boy or a girl?—Would it have his hair, or her eyes? His sharp chin, or her button nose?

He would find out quite soon – for Penelope Smith burst into the room, interrupting his imagination. Her eyes glittered with excitement and, perhaps, some tears. "Oh, congratulations, Your Highness! Quickly, Sir, the Princess is asking for you. And Earl Portsmouth as well. Both of you, this way, please."

Alexander was out the room before Emmett could pick David up. He rushed into the room where he saw his wife in a birthing chair, dripping with perspiration and a baby in her arms. The midwives tended to her, tittering about the child as they went. Her hair was a mess, with a few strands sticking to her shining forehead, and she had not an ounce of powder on her face; but her eyes shone and her face was more radiant than he'd ever seen it, and she was more beautiful than ever before.

"Oh, Alex," she said, still short of breath, "it's a boy. We said we'd name him William, didn't we?"

"We did," he agreed, coming to stand by her and gingerly running a hand across her forehead. "Oh, beloved, you must be so tired. It sounded horrible from the next room."

"It was horrible," she agreed, laughing, "the most pain I've ever experienced. But this baby – our William...oh, he is worth every bit of it and more. Just look at him, Alexander, what an angel."

"An angel indeed. He takes after his mother." He leaned down to press a kiss to her forehead, and then, with additional caution, to his newborn son's.

"All right, Emmeline darling, give me the child. You must rest and be tended to," Bethany trilled, coming to take her great-nephew from Emmeline's arms. The newborn began to squirm and cry immediately. "There, there, William. Great-aunt Bethany is here. Hush now."

Baby William quietened down quickly enough. The older woman began to shoo everyone out of the room. Alexander was reluctant to leave his wife, but a firm glare from the marchioness was persuasion enough, and he squeezed Emmeline's hand before exiting the room with everyone else.

"That man loves you, you know," Bethany said, smiling. "I know you didn't come together in the best of ways, and – and I am still sorry for what I did and what I caused...I am sorry for being blind to what you wanted, and thinking that I knew what was best for you. But I am not sorry that you married him."

Emmeline smiled back, her contentment written all over her face. "Neither am I, Aunt Beth. Neither am I."

A/N Thank you so much for reading! Vote, comment and share, and look out for part two, coming soon!

# Chapter Thirty - PART TWO

------------------------------------------------------------

A/N H-A-P-P-Y F-R-I-D-A-Y! This is part two of what ought to be three of Chapter Thirty...or maybe there'll be four parts, depending on how the story runs its course (or rather how much I can't let it go...h aha). It's definitely coming to an end, though, and I hope you enjoy these last few updates :) x Leanne

"PRINCESS DIANNA," A MAID CALLED FROM OUTSIDE QUEEN EMMELINE'S study, where the mother of three sat explaining the intricacies of balancing business and pleasure to her children, "you have a visitor to see you, please, Your Highness."

"Come in, please," Emmeline replied, and the maid entered the room.

"Another gentleman caller, no doubt?" the youngest of the three St James siblings, Lucas, clarified with a teasing glint in his eye. He had fair hair and his mother's green eyes, bearing a striking resemblance to his maternal grandmother Anne. His features were softer than his cousin David's and his older brother William's, but albeit his lack of fierce masculinity in his outward appearance there was a certain liveliness and charm about him his brother lacked, that made young ladies swoon just at the sight of him.

Some girls devoted unhealthy amounts of time to discussing which of the princes was better looking, and though all of their parents preferred the crown prince simply because of his status, there were a large number of young ladies across the land who favoured Lucas.

"Pray do not tease Anna so," William chided, his voice far more solemn than his younger brother's, as it always was. His prominent cheekbones, sharp jaw, jet black hair and cool blue eyes lent him an air of regality fit for a future king. "You know she detests it, and Mother hates the pair of you rowing."

"I can stand up for myself, Will," the blonde-haired middle child and sole princess Dianna interjected. Then, glaring at her younger brother with her piercing blue eyes, the pair she shared with her older brother and her father, "I actually think it a compliment I have suitors to call on me, Lucas!"

"As if there isn't a long line of ladies begging me to marry them," was the response. "Besides, I don't play with their hearts, unlike a certain someone."

"I do not toy with them," she huffed, indignant.

"You absolutely do," Lucas disagreed, grinning. "You let the last one buy you five bouquets of red roses before telling him you'd only ever been interested in being friends, and the one before that, well, we all know he ran out sobbing."

"He was not sobbing!" she shouted. "You are such a—"

"No shouting, Dianna, please," Emmeline cut in sharply. "And Lucas, I wish you wouldn't rile your sister up like that. Like your brother said, you knew it would lead to an argument."

"I'm going to see to my guest," the princess said, standing from her chair with another huff. "I will see you at dinner, Mother, and you as well, William."

With nothing to offer to her younger brother as a means of goodbye but a glare sharp enough to slit his throat, she turned to leave the room.

"Dianna, my dear?" her mother called after her just as she was about to step out the door.

"Yes, Mother?" she turned her head so that her mother could speak to her.

"Be upfront with this young man. Don't break another heart."

"Yes, Mother," she grumbled, and then she left the room, but not before shooting another glare at her younger brother, who was smugly reclined in his chair and smirking triumphantly at her.

***

As usual, do vote, comment, and share!!! Your support means everything to me <3

# Chapter Thirty - PART THREE

------------------------------------------------------------

A/N We're finally here – the last update on Apollo. So, this ended up longer than I intended it to be, but for some reason I get the feeling that you guys won't complain about it, haha. So for the very last time, here's this week's update – enjoy!!!

WHEN THEY FINISHED WITH THEIR OFFICIAL BUSINESS HE STOOD TO GO, bowing respectfully as he was expected to do before his queen. "I shall take my leave now, Your Majesty. Thank you for your time."

"Wait." She heard herself speak before she even knew she had opened her mouth. Then, with more control over her own words, she asked, "Will you...Will you stay for tea, Admiral? It is about to be teatime, and I imagine you are hungry."

"I suppose I cannot refuse a royal decree, Madam," he jested, the corners of his eyes crinkling. "Thank you, then. I will stay."

Emmeline rang a bell and called for macarons and their finest pot of tea, and momentarily though they were both grey and old now they found themselves returning to the days of their youth, the first time they had taken their tea together in Lockhart Manor all the way in Portsmouth.

This memory struck Peter with a thought.

"How is your brother, Madam?—How is Duke Mayfair?"

"He is well, the last I heard from him. It has been a week or so since he last wrote," she replied. "His wife Victoria – unfortunately she left us a number of years back, but he has recovered mostly from it. When she passed away he moved to live in London, in Wellington House where my father used to be. It isn't far from here; would you like to call on him?—We could go together, I do miss him."

"That would be agreeable," he answered with a measured smile. "Madam—"

"Please, Emmeline will suffice," she interrupted. "This is no longer official business, and I think, Peter, that we are rather above such frivolous formality."

"Well, yes...Emmeline." He smiled at her, though his tone still betrayed some unease. He hesitated briefly before asking, "Are you happy? Married to His Majesty?"

She paused to consider it, and found herself wondering how they would have been if they had ended up marrying. Would she be happier?—Was there a chance that their relationship could have fallen apart, just as quickly as it came to be? Her relationship with Alexander had never been quite as emotionally charged as hers with Peter had been, but it was stable at least, built on the solid foundation of a good friendship, and it had lasted well through the years. Yet was the ideal relationship one like that – not volatile, but never extremely passionate either? Or was it just the thought of young love that had made her romance with Peter feel so exciting?

She would never know.

"Quite," she answered eventually. "He has rather grown on me. We never did have anything as intense as what I had with you..."—she took a breath to calm her heart—"but we are happy."

"That is good to hear."

"And you?—Is there any lucky lady I should know about?"

"No, no, just the ocean and my men," he laughed. "I was – and am – happy a bachelor. My work has given me meaning, as it always has, and I am very content with where I am."

"I'm glad." She smiled at him then, and it was genuine. "I suppose we may call ourselves friends?"

"Yes, of course," he answered. "If you ever have anything I could possibly help with, please write to me. I will leave you my address before I go."

"Well, then the same must go for you, Peter," she said. "Please never stand on ceremony. You still have a place in my heart, and if you need anything that all, I promise I will do my best to help you."

"Thank you." He smiled. "Oh, Emmeline, these macarons are—"

He was likely about to pay her chef a compliment when a knock on the door interrupted him. Emmeline sighed at the interruption.

Nonetheless, she called out, "Who is it?"

"Mother, it's us!"

"Come in," she relented, sighing again, and Peter chuckled at the exhaustion her face betrayed the moment she heard the energetic response from her younger son. Before he could comment on it, however, in tumbled three handsome young men, two of them princes and one an earl. The

Admiral rose in greeting, and, out of respect for her guest, Emmeline stood as well.

"What are you three rascals doing here? Are you not supposed to be with Alexander?" she asked, brows knitted sternly together.

The oldest of the three, with Victoria Arden's thick chocolate locks and dark brown eyes, spoke first with a mischievous grin. "We're sorry, Aunt Emmeline, we just heard from Aunt Penny that your old suitor came calling, and we absolutely had to see what man had you so enchanted back then."

"Do not speak so disrespectfully, David. Any guest to the palace deserves all our utmost respect, not to mention a gentleman who has been of such great service to our country," Emmeline chided sharply. "Children, this is Admiral Peter Jamison."

"Admiral." The second oldest bowed immediately, his voice far more solemn than his cousin's.

"Prince William." He greeted in return, bowing respectfully the man who might one day be his king, depending on his longevity and King Alexander's.

"Admiral Jamison," the younger prince echoed, also bowing.

"Prince Lucas." The admiral returned the pleasantry. "How are you, Your Highnesses, Your Lordship?"

"We are all very well, Admiral, thank you," William replied with a nod, not smiling. "And you?"

"I am well, Your Highness, thank you."

"Very good. Now, David, you will be going home to your father tonight?" Emmeline asked her nephew, looking far more pleased with the three young men.

"Yes, Aunt," he answered. "I am only due to return to Portsmouth in a week."

"Well, then, Admiral Jamison, how would you fancy going to Wellington House with him?" she offered. "I'm sure Emmett would love to see you."

"Father would indeed," David agreed, his welcoming smile reaching his eyes. "And I would be honoured to have you as well, Admiral. I must also apologise if my jesting earlier was interpreted as a lack of esteem, I assure you I have nothing but respect for you."

Peter chuckled, accepting the young earl's words with a smile and a comment that his was exceedingly similar to his father in mannerism. Queen Emmeline watched on, beaming all the while. Emmett had raised this boy well – while David had the same playful tendencies the now much-aged Duke Mayfair once did, he also had the same genuineness and politeness his father had.

That evening the three were on their way to Wellington House. She would be spending the night on her brother's estate for the first time in a number of months, and Alexander decided not to accompany her this time although he usually did when she visited the Lockharts' London property. Instead he had said that he would stay with the children in the palace, and bade her goodbye with a kiss to her forehead.

Emmett was, as anticipated, elated to see his old friend.

"Peter, what a surprise!" he cried when he opened the main door, deciding to go as far as to offer him a brotherly embrace. He had expected only to see his son, but there stood not just David, but also his sister and the man whom he had, for so many years, considered his dearest friend.

The Admiral laughed and returned the hug.

"Indeed, it is marvellous to see you again."

"Emmeline, thank you for bringing him over," the duke exclaimed. "I could not imagine a better guest to spend my evening with. Come in, come in. Have you had dinner?"

"We have, thank you, Emmett," Emmeline replied, smiling. "Perhaps we might talk in the drawing room?"

"Of course," he agreed. "You look well, Peter. I heard about your promotions over the years – how do you fancy being an admiral...?"

As they walked they talked about times old and new, times bright and blue. They sat down and talked more yet. All three felt young again, even as they all had deep lines running across their faces and heads of silver hair. They reminisced through the night, wanting to be in each other's company for as long as they could be.

Over the courses of their lives, nothing had gone as any of them had thought it would. They had feuded and cried and grieved back then. They had loved and lost and their hearts had all bled for it. But all three of them were satisfied with where providence had taken them. The dramatics of their youth seemed only to be old bedtime stories now, all the unpleasant memories blurred by time and irrelevant to the present moment.

While they chatted endlessly the sun set and the sun rose again, and they were happy.

* THE END *